BRONX SAVAGES

Lock Down Publications and Ca$h
Presents
BRONX SAVAGES
A Novel by *Romell Tukes*

Bronx Savages

Lock Down Publications
Po Box 944
Stockbridge, Ga 30281

Visit our website @
www.lockdownpublications.com

Lock Down Publications
Like our page on Facebook: Lock Down Publications @
www.facebook.com/lockdownpublications.ldp
Book interior design by: **Shawn Walker**
Edited by: **Kiera Northington**

Stay Connected with Us!

Text **LOCKDOWN** to 22828 to stay up-to-date with new releases,
sneak peaks, contests and more…
Thank you.

Submission Guideline.

Submit the first three chapters of your completed manuscript to ldpsubmissions@gmail.com, subject line: Your book's title. The manuscript must be in a .doc file and sent as an attachment. Document should be in Times New Roman, double spaced and in size 12 font. Also, provide your synopsis and full contact information. If sending multiple submissions, they must each be in a separate email.

Have a story but no way to send it electronically? You can still submit to LDP/Ca$h Presents. Send in the first three chapters, written or typed, of your completed manuscript to:

LDP: Submissions Dept
Po Box 944
Stockbridge, Ga 30281

DO NOT send original manuscript. Must be a duplicate.

Provide your synopsis and a cover letter containing your full contact information.

Thanks for considering LDP and Ca$h Presents.

Romell Tukes

Chapter 1

Soundview, The Bronx

"When I was your age, my father killed a nigga right in front of me in the back yard of our home in Mount Vernon, and since that day I look at life different," Moss told his son, who soaked up every word he said, while lying in his bedroom he shared with his sleeping little brother.

"Why?" Nick asked, looking at his dad's heavy rope chain, which he wanted so bad.

"Why did it change me, or why did he kill the man?"

"Both, Daddy?" Nick said with his ten-year-old voice.

"While my father was a different type of breed, he murdered men for nothing, his heart was cold."

"Ohhh."

"I don't know how your life will turn out when you grow up, but if you follow the family business, I want you to know one thing and live by it." Moss' words were very stern and straight.

"Ok."

"Always look a man in the eyes before you kill him."

"Ohh."

"To show honor." Nick's words made his father smile like a proud parent.

"Yes, now go to sleep and tomorrow, I'll take you out to the gun range."

"I got school tomorrow."

"You can afford to miss a day," Moss stated, getting up to leave his son's room.

"Good night," Nick yelled before tucking himself in the cartoon sheets and blanket.

Moss walked to the master bedroom, which was down the hall-way. They lived in a nice area in between Castle Hill and Soundview, on a block called Taylor Avenue. The house had an upstairs and downstairs four bedrooms, two bathrooms, a nice kitchen and backyard space.

Once in the room, he could hear the shower running, which meant his beautiful wife Jalisa, the woman he'd been married to for years now, was in there. When they met at a party in Westchester County where Jalisa was going to college, the two of them clicked and shit took off from there.

Now at thirty and with three kids, their love life was even stranger than most, the only difference being their lifestyles.

Jalisa works for a high-class bank in Manhattan while Moss is a contract killer, some would call a hitman. It took years for Jalisa to even figure out what her man did for a living, until one day she decided to trail him and see why his private life was so private.

That night, she witnessed her first murder in Harlem, in front of a project building on the Eastside. When confronting him about it days later, he told her the truth. "Killing is my real job." Not even a day later, Jalisa found out she was pregnant with their first daughter, Brooklyn.

Moss followed his father Rah Rah's footsteps into the family's murder-for-hire business, something rare in this day and age, but he became lucky enough to meet some powerful people throughout his years.

Growing up as a kid in the Bronx, he knew there wouldn't be too many options of being very successful besides sports, rapping, selling drugs or owning a business.

As a twenty-one-year-old young man, Rah Rah got deported to Jamaica, six bodies found disposed of in the truck of his Town car. Moss hadn't heard from his dad since. But last year, one of his cousins informed him there were rumors of the government killing Rah Rah in prison, due to his past out there.

Moss didn't have a strong relationship with his dad, but he did pick up a lot of jewels and acknowledge him. Luckily, his mom Pamala did well at raising him and the rest of his brothers and sisters.

"Babe, you still up?" Jalisa walked out the bathroom lotion glowing.

Jalisa was eye candy. Slim-thick and curvy, light brown eyes, with dimples, white teeth and beautiful to her core.

"I was waiting on you, love."

"For what? My period just come on, so you not getting none of this coochie tonight. I'm sorry." Jalisa laughed, putting on her panties and night clothes.

"You know I'm nasty."

"That's why you sleeping on the couch with your nasty ass. I know how y'all Jamaicans is," she joked, climbing in the bed with him, as his long dreads freely relaxed on the pillow.

"What time are you going to work tomorrow?"

"Early, why?"

"Just asking. I don't want you to put Nick on the bus, I want him to come with me."

"Babe, you know he got school and should not be around that shit." Jalisa saw what Moss was trying to do and she frowned upon it, but at the same time she didn't want her son to be a punk or dumb to the streets.

Jalisa's whole family from Brooklyn was cold-blooded gangstas but she really wanted more for her family.

"Let me raise him right. I know what I'm doing, tha boy gonna be a real man one day," Moss said before she laid her head down on his chiseled chest and fell asleep.

***

Bronxville, NY

Instead of attending school today, Nick rode in the passenger seat of his dad's Cadillac truck, listening to Biggie Smalls, nodding his head.

Spending time with Moss made little Nick appreciate him, more even if he had to skip school for the day. Nick didn't hate school, nor did he love it, but he did do enough to mainly get by.

"Whatever you see today, I want you to never repeat or even think about it again." Moss tuned down the music so his little man could hear him as soon as they arrived at a rundown auto shop.

"Of course, Daddy."

"Good, now stay a few feet behind me." Moss got out, tucking a pistol and looking around to make sure his coast was clear.

The front door was open, so Moss made his way inside as Nick slowly got out, thinking if he should just stay in the car.

"Tato, where are you at?" Moss yelled, seeing there was only one man in the area working on a car.

"The boss man is in the back. How can I help you?" the employee stated, getting off the floor to see Moss now aiming a weapon at him.

"Wrong place, wrong time," Moss told him before pulling the trigger twice as bullets went through his skull.

Nick couldn't believe he just witnessed his first murder. He couldn't move a muscle, he only stared as Moss now walked to the back to see Tato rushing out his office with a suitcase and running right into Moss' chest.

"Ross, err... Moss, good to see you." Tato was so scared he forgot Moss' name temporarily, but he'd heard some horrible stories about the man with the cold stare, who wore the long dreadlocks.

"You didn't keep your word to my boss, now look what's about to happen, you had one man already killed," said Moss.

"I can make it right." Tato cried like a bitch hoping it would work, but instead it backfired.

"Crying is for bitches... do you bleed once a month?"

"No, I'm sorry. I need more time," Tato pleaded, looking at Nick peeping his head through his office door.

"Your time is up."

BOOM....

BOOM....

BOOM....

BOOM....

The echo was so loud it could be heard from outside in the middle of the block.

"Let's go," Moss said, seeing his son had cold feet.

"Is he gonna be ok?" Nick asked a question he already knew the answer to.

"He'll be ok, trust me." Moss tapped his son on the back before walking him to a play station.

Seeing a dead body made Nick fear Moss more than anything so he would always remember this day.

Romell Tukes

Chapter 2

Manhattan, NY

Mark's office was located in one of the tallest buildings downtown. He was the sixth biggest accountant in the state of New York with his own firm. Most people thought he was a white boy because of his blue eyes and blonde hair and also the upbeat attitude he kept, but Mark's mom is Puerto Rican, and his dad is white.

He grew up around money, so being rich and flashy was all he knew. Nobody would have ever guessed Mark lived a second life, not even his beautiful wife. Outside of running the company, Mark was one of the biggest drug dealers in the city and he would get a nigga's whole family killed. With hitters like Moss on his team, he could take on any NY crew or take over any block.

The light knock at his door startled him as he turned around from staring off into the city clouds outside his window.

"Come in," he yelled to see the pretty young clerk he'd just hired walk in.

"A guy by the name of Mr. Moss is here to see you, but I don't see him on your schedule, sir," she stated, looking at a clipboard with her glasses on.

"It's cool to let him in. And how about we go out to dinner tonight?"

"Me?" she replied, shocked that a handsome man like Mark would want to take her out.

"Yes… you, my love. Join me for dinner not as your boss, but let's say a friend," he stated.

"Ok, sure." The clerk rushed out happily as Moss walked inside wearing a blazer and slacks.

"Moss, good to see you, boss man," said Mark as Moss sat down and placed his feet on the desk as if he owned the place, not giving a fuck how Mark felt.

"You got my money?" Moss' words were short and straight to the point.

"I do, don't I always?"

"Yes, but I don't have to always come and get it."

"True, but I needed to see you, so I figured to kill two birds with one stone."

"What's on your mind."

"There is a man giving me a lot of problems and I need your help." In his head, Mark already knew Moss' answer.

"How much?"

"You can name the price, but this job is going to be a little different and harder, Moss" said Mark, with a cold stare.

"I'm not understanding."

"The person I need killed is a very powerful man, Moss."

"Ok, who is he?"

"The chief of police," Mark said, before the whole room got silent.

"You sure?"

"Yes, he's fucking up my money and I think the fucker is on to me."

"This is a big hit, we are talking about here, boss man," Moss hit him with his words.

"Okay, how about two hundred thousand?"

"No, please don't disrespect me like that bro, real shit."

"What's your price?"

" A half-million dollars and nothing less, my guy."

"Shit." Mark had the money but didn't want to spend that much on him to make the kill, but it had to be done.

"Give me a few days."

"Ok, done deal and I'll be waiting for money to hit," Moss responded, getting up.

"I'll have it sent to you soon."

"Who is it anyway?"

"Santanza."

"Are you kidding me?" Moss knew him too well, because he'd sent Moss upstate to prison for five years when he was eighteen years old.

"Not at all."

"Alright, I'm on it."

"Thank you," Mark said, hoping this played out well.

***

West Bronx

Nick sat in class, thinking about the two men he witnessed being killed the other day. Truth be told, he hadn't slept since that day. But he would never tell his dad, because the last thing he wanted to do is look like a little pussy bitch, something Moss hated.

"Nick, could you answer that math question for me, since you look so eager to learn today?" the teacher Mrs. Bella asked, sitting in front of his class.

"I'm sorry. I forgot the problem," Nick replied.

"That's because it wasn't a problem. I just wanted to show the class what happens if you don't listen," said Mrs. Bella before the bell rang, ending the class.

Nick hated fifth grade, but he could do nothing about it. Luckily, his crew helped him look forward to the end of the school year. Summer was fast approaching, and they made plans to have fun every day of the summer.

He and his boys loved riding bikes, going to parks, and talking to the local girls their age.

"Nick," two voices shouted from behind him in the crowded hallway.

"Yo, Top and Ray, what's up? I didn't see either one of you today when my mom dropped me off out front."

"We was late, my dad had to bring us to school," Ray the nerdy one outta the bunch replied.

"This nigga mom was too high to drop us off as always," Top shouted out, because he spent the night over at his first cousin Ray's house.

"You knew that before you came." Ray gave him a look, but Nick already knew Ray's mom was a crackhead. He went over to his house daily to catch smoking bases.

"Let's go to lunch," Nick said.

"Good, I'm starving," Ray replied as he made his way to the lunchroom.

"That girl asked where you were yesterday when I was at football practice," Top said as they walked into the packed lunchroom. Top was the school quarterback.

"Who?" Nick already had a clue, but he played it cool.

"Hope, she is a cheerleader. I forgot she was the captain."

"Oh. I don't know why she is asking about me because I hate her," Nick said, hearing them laugh because everybody knew they liked each other.

Nick and Hope lived in the same area and their families were very close, but Nick never expressed to anybody how much he really cared for her.

Chapter 3

Manhattan, NY

Jalisa worked as a bank teller in the most upscale bank in the city. Moss got her the job years ago and to this day, she had no clue how and never questioned it because Jalisa knew how connected her man was.

The day was long and dragging at three p.m. She felt the bottom of her feet already swollen in her high heels. Dealing with a bunch of high-class white people was the worst, because they had no respect until you checked them.

With two more hours left at work, she played the clock while doing money transfers and bank referrals.

"Excuse me," an old woman in front of the counter shouted as if Jalisa had a hearing problem.

"I can hear you, Miss. How can I help you today?" Jalisa responded respectfully.

"Add this check to my overseas account and deposit the other check into my business account please," the wrinkled face woman requested with a rude demeanor, making Jalisa feel a little awkward and uncomfortable.

"How much is the check? Because past twelve o'clock, we can't deposit any funds over a million dollars, cash or check." Jalisa saw the woman's face frown.

"Well, this is two million and I've done it before, maybe you don't know who I am."

"Excuse me, did I hear that correctly?" Jalisa tried her best to keep her cool.

"All you have to do is deposit the checks and go home to your project building, because with one phone call, I will have your job. I know the owner at this company," the older woman shouted, making people behind her in line pay close attention.

Right when Jalisa was about to respond and curse the racist bitch out, her co-worker Ashley saw something on the check.

"Jalisa, this check is a fake. Look at the bar codes, it's missing lines and the numbers are off," Ashley pointed out.

When the old white woman saw she was caught, her feet reversed and she got outta there so fast, Jalisa and Ashley started to die laughing, along with the civilians behind them.

***

49th Precinct, The Bronx

Santanza, made it back in his office after his interview and sat down with the mayor, to discuss stopping drugs coming in and out of The Bronx. For a few months now the city violence had been mostly all due to drug sales and dealing in his city.

Being from Queens and raised in a Puerto Rican household, Santanza and his two brothers took an oath to be successful in life and not like their dope fiend father, who spend most of his life in jail fucking up because he couldn't stop getting high.

One of his younger brothers got hooked on dope and was now a homeless man on the corner, begging for money to eat and get high.

Luckily, his other brother Phill had just recently become a detective and worked his ass off to take care of his newborn.

Santanza had a wife and three kids. His wife's father is the mayor of New York, so they had a good bond and a good relationship overall.

The main problem going on right now is Santanza believes a very worthy powerful man by the name of Mark is flooding his city with drugs, and he's about to be law enforcement's number-one target.

Thanks to a few snitches, Santanza was able to piece everything together and got it right. Now his attention was on Mark and finding out more of his operations at the moment.

Santanza had his own way of working, he would first start from the head, then work his way down to the feet.

Webster PJ's, The Bronx

"How much you got?" Ice asked the young man from Brooklyn, who came all the way down to re-up with Ice, who was known to have the best work in the city.

"I need eight keys."

"Don't you still owe me twenty?" Ice remembered from last time.

"I got that too, son."

Iight good, so let me get that shit then, bruh." Ice didn't play about his money at all.

"Dis everything in the bag." The young man handed the money over to him in the staircase of one of the most dangerous projects in The Bronx.

"Your brother Snow owed me a hundred grand before he went upstate and word is, he is telling now." Ice caught the young man off guard, because Snow was the one who put him on to Ice a few months ago, and shit was going good.

"Bro, I don't know nothing about y'all business or what he doing, I'm just trying do good business wit you." The young brother saw a smirk appear on Ice, face feeling something was about to go left real quick.

"The sad shit is you are your brother's keeper," Ice said before pulling out a weapon.

"I can get you that money Snow owes, just give me a few days, please. I'll take care of it."

"Too late, son." Ice fired four bullets into the man's face, killing him before going back upstairs to count the money. Ice was Moss' younger brother and a killer. He loved to get money so he could life a fast, flashy life unlike Moss, but the two both had tha killing instinct.

Romell Tukes

Chapter 4

Westside, The Bronx

Today, Moss felt like picking up his son from school to spend some time with him before he took care of the hit later on tonight,

Moss pulled up, blasting old school R&B. Mint Condition, one of his favorite groups of all time. He saw Nick coming out of the school building playing with his friend. Moss knew all of them, but he didn't approve of them because they were too soft.

BEEP…. BEEP….

When Nick heard the horn blow, he looked to see his dad's SUV and rushed towards it like a football player about to blast.

"Dad, what are you doing here?"

"I came to get you from school, what it look like, big head?"

"Oh, you're gonna get my brother and sister too?" Nick asked because they all went to different schools in the borough.

"Your mother already picked them up. Now are you gonna ask a hundred questions or get in." Moss knew his son wouldn't stop the dumb questions.

"Can my friends come?"

"No, now get your little black ass inside the car before I leave you with them," Moss told him and saw Nick wave his goodbye to his friends.

Nick climbed inside, nodding his head to the old school beats he knew nothing about.

"How was school?" Moss asked, turning down the music as he bent corners.

"Good, I passed two tests and shit." Nick slipped up and didn't even realize he cursed until Moss punched him in his frail chest, taking the wind out of him.

"Sorry."

"Don't let it happen again. Are you hungry or not?"

"Yes, they had tuna salad for lunch. It was so nasty, but I ate it anyway."

"I bet, but you know I love you right?" Moss' question somewhat caught Nick off guard, he didn't know to reply.

"Yes."

"Your mom, brother and sister are my love and heart. If anything ever happens to me, you will become the man of the house and that comes with a lot of weight," Moss explained as he pulled in front of a pizza shop owned by some Italians he'd known for years and had done work for.

"I'm smart, Daddy. I can take care of the family." Nick's words made Moss smile ear to ear.

"That's good to know. Now let's go eat some pizza, and no pork." Moss knew all his kids liked pork, but he tried to break them outta that mode.

***

Kingsbridge, The Bronx

Santanza was on his way to meet up with a special informant he'd known for years. The two went to school together and grew up on the same block, but they chose different paths.

He pulled up in front of a brick building to see Flacc coming out with his gold chains and watches. Flacc was a big-time drug dealer, one of the biggest in Kingsbridge, so nobody would ever imagine him being a rat.

"What's up, boss man?" Flacc joked, climbing into the Tahoe SUV, looking around and checking his surroundings.

"I need news."

"Ok, there is a guy named Mark, some rich business owner from Manhattan. I just found out he supplies my connect on Broadway and word is this guy ain't nothing to fuck with." Flacc saw Santanza's eyes light up as he pulled off to spin the block.

"This is the fucker I've been looking into! I knew it!" Santanza shouted with happiness, pulling over to drop off his childhood friend.

"So now can you tell the police in the Heights to leave my people alone?" was Flacc's only request.

"I got you, no problem. I'll take care of it tonight...you have my word."

"Thanks." Flacc got out and walked up the block praying what he just revealed would never get back to him

It was close to ten at night so the streets were dark. Flacc's sister lived down the block, but he had a few stash houses all around the area. Being in his late forties, he'd made an oath to get out the game this year, but it was all he'd known.

Walking past a dark alley, he thought he heard a noise but he paid it no mind, until the footsteps behind him sped up and someone grabbed his whole neck, forcing him into the alley.

Romell Tukes

Chapter 5

Soundview, The Bronx

Next night

Moss got dressed in all black, headed downstairs in his living room, thinking about Santanza and the mission tonight.

"Bae, you coming to bed?" Jalisa startled him coming downstairs in a silk robe.

"Huh, my love?" Moss discreetly slid the weapon under the couch before she could see it. He always tried his best to keep his family and people outta his business, because he believed in the less the better, at trial.

"I thought you were sleep, honey." Jalisa looked around to see Moss' gym bag which he only used for his dirty work.

"Sorry, I couldn't sleep," he lied, and she caught the energy.

"I see why now." Jalisa crossed her arms.

"Come on, my love. I have to step out for a second. I'll be back in no time." He gave her a look of guarantee.

"Ok, give me a kiss." Jalisa gave her man a deep passionate kiss as always.

"I love you. I'ma be back before it's time to take them to school."

"You better, because Nick gonna be looking for you and Mickey so be here," she said, switching away and showing off her beautiful curves most women would die for.

Moss finished getting dressed and made his way outside to his hooptie he used to get around in when it's time to kill.

The ride to Pelham wasn't too far, only a few minutes away, but he took the long route just to plan his hit again. The chance of Santanza having cameras around his home was a most likely, so Moss just decided to lay on him.

***

Santanza woke up at 5:30 am, ready to start his day, leaving his wife sleeping as he did every morning. His wife Jessica was a lawyer for the city.

After showering, brushing his teeth and making coffee, he was ready to get dressed and leave for work. Santanza planned to stay out a little late and have a little fun with his side chick, who recently started at the police station.

Leaving out the house, he made sure to lock the door, but he didn't see the gunman behind him with a pistol.

"You fucking move, it's over, bitch nigga." Moss scared him as Santanza froze in his tracks.

"This ain't what you want to do, trust me, just walk away please."

"Sorry boss, but I'm calling the shots here, and today you're outta luck." Moss' voice sounded cold blooded.

"Who sent you? Let's talk about it for a second. I'm sure this is a mistake," Santanza stated calmly, hoping he could sweet talk his way outta this.

"It's over, but nice try."

"Leave my wife outta this at least, that's all I request."

"Will do," Moss said before pulling the trigger.

BLOC....

BLOC....

Santanza's body fell into a flowerpot and Moss fired two shots in his chest, then walked off hearing someone inside rush downstairs.

Moss saw the victim's wife rush to open the door and he was about to kill her, but Moss fired a few live rounds into the air to scare her off, instead of killing her.

***

Manhattan, NY

Mark had a big grin on his face as he watched the news report the death of The Bronx's police chief this morning outside his home. Mark really wanted to jump up and down, but he held it down like a champ thinking about his next move. One thing he could trust was Moss cleaning his dirty work, so Mark had no worries of nothing getting back to him, not one bite.

Leaning back in his chair, the office door flew wide open as if the police kicked it in.

"Where the fuck my money?" Moss spoke in a malicious tone.

"I was sending it right now, Moss, I swear to God." Mark logged into his computer then he turned it towards Moss so he could see the transfer.

"You was? Oh," Moss stated, putting up his weapon.

"Yes, it's been a busy day up here for me, I'm telling you."

"Did you watch the news?" Moss asked, sitting down like he owned the place.

"Good job. I knew you would show your ass and put his ass down," boasted Mark.

"This is everyday shit, but I'ma lay low for a little while," Moss said, getting up to leave before reminding Mark his money better be there within thirty minutes.

***

Soundview, The Bronx

Nick and Top played the game system in his house after school, something they did every day, rather than at Top's crib or Ray's house, where his crackhead mother was there begging them for money.

"I bet you like five times," Top bragged about how he beat his boy at *2K Basketball* on PlayStation.

"Man, you got lucky again and I know you got the cheat codes locked in your head," Nick joked.

"Take your loss like a man, sucker."

"Whatever stupid, but I want to change my name," Nick paused the game, giving his own comment deep thought.

"Why?"

"Nick sounds too gay and I'm bout to be eleven years old in a few weeks."

"I like my nickname."

"They call you Top because of the size of your head," Nick shot out slapping him on his head.

"If you want to change it, then we gotta make it catchy."

"How about Murder One?"

"My cousin's boyfriend's name is that from Brooklyn and he is doing twenty-five to life in prison right now," Top shot back, not liking the name at all.

"How about Killa Kill?"

"That's not too bad, but why do you want all deadly names, just to get a regular name like Chip or Lace?" Top suggested.

"Nah, too regular." Nick didn't want to tell Top about the murder he saw his dad commit, which made him eager to change his name.

"Bodies be dropping all over. Why would you change your mind to a villain name?" Top seemed confused.

"That's it."

"What?" Top thought Nick lost his mind.

"I'm changing my name to Body."

"Huh?"

"Call me Body from now on. I no longer will answer to Nick," said Nick with a serious look.

"Iight little Nick."

"Stop playing, bro, it's Body."

"My bad. Body, nice to meet you, sir. Now let me bust your ass in basketball right now." Top unpaused the game and continue to whip Body's ass in *2K*.

Chapter 6

Queens, NY

Ice came out to meet his main supplier, Papa, a Dominican man with pull all over the city and the Dominican Republic, which of course was his home.

The past week had been a blessing for Ice because he was able to open a new block in the Uptown section of Gun Hill, with a few Jamaicans he'd known since they were kids.

Papa wanted this money today. Ice had been owing for some time now, so he was a little nervous because everybody who knew the little man, knew he didn't play about family or money.

Walking into the smoke shop, Ice saw a few Spanish cats posted up, acting like they were busy filling shit, but Ice knew better. The men were all there for Papa and his protection.

"Papa?" Ice asked the young man, who looked at his bag.

"We gotta check the bag first, Papa." A tall Spanish cat started coming around the counter with a TEC-9 submachine gun hanging from a strap around his neck.

"Iight." Ice opened up the bag and showed it to Papa's nephew, who he saw every trip.

"You good, papi. He in the back, awaiting you right now." Papa's nephew stated after seeing the bag was only filled with money.

Ice slowly walked to the back to see Papa relaxing, sitting in the dark with a candle.

"My good friend, Ice. I truly thought you would forget about me," Papi's voice was very low and scary.

"Why would you think that? We have a great business relationship?" Ice placed the money on the table.

"Yes, but you delayed the meeting twice and you know what happens after the third miss?" Papa faced him with a smirk.

"Yeah, that's why I'm here with extra for that and I need ten keys of dope."

"I hope it's ten keys' worth of money in there?" Papa's English started to sound perfect whenever he spoke about money.

"Everything is in the bag."

"Ok, I like what I see, but how's the family, Ice?" Papa asked a question he never asked.

"Great, why do you ask?"

"Just checking, but I'll have my nephew call you when he's ready to drop off the ten keys to you. Enjoy the day, Ice." Papa did a friendly dismissal, but it wasn't sitting right with Ice, but he focused back on his bag, thinking about what he was going to do with the dope coming to him.

***

South Bronx

Two weeks later

Body, as the world called him now, celebrated his eleventh birthday in a large park with friends and family on a nice sunny day.

"Hey birthday boy," Hope said, approaching Body from behind, shocking him.

"What are you doing here?" Body tried to hide his happiness by putting on a mean face, but Hope knew him too well.

"Thanks for the non-invite, but my mom and my mom are still close, so she told us to come today," Hope said over the loud music, flashing her bright hazel eyes.

"Oh, cool." Body saw Top coming, so he acted as if Hope wasn't even there.

"Body, what's up? Let's go play basketball real quick, everybody came out today," said Top, taking a fast look at Hope, then back to his boy.

"Who's Body?" Hope asked them.

"That's what everybody calls me now, including you, from now on." Body made sure he said it with his chest.

"Ok, sure… well, I'll see y'all later. I'm going kick it with Chanell," Hope said, walking off laughing at Nick's new name.

"She is feeling you, brodee," Top told Body, catching his stare also.

"Whatever. I wonder where my dad is, he is supposed to be here." Body saw his mom coming from afar with her sister.

"Your pops be busy all day, bro. What the heck he does again?"

"Run a business."

"What kind?"

"I don't know. Stop asking so much shit," Body shot back because he didn't know a lot about his dad's job besides, he made good money.

"You think when I get older, he'll get me a job?" Top asked.

"Maybe." Body's mom and Auntie Dawn stopped in front of them both.

"What y'all doing?" Auntie Dawn stated, chewing gum and acting ratchet as always.

"Waiting on my dad," Body replied.

"He should be here shortly with your gift, Body. Now come have fun," Jalisa said, calling her son by his requested name.

"Did you just call his little dirty ass Body?" Auntie Dawn said.

"Yeah, that's his nickname, he said."

"Oh Lord, another Moss," his Aunt Dawn said before walking off.

"Come enjoy your party," Jalisa told the boys as they followed her to the small party.

***

Fordham Road, The Bronx

Moss talked to the salesperson at the dirt bike store, trying to get a good price on a nice size dirt bike for Nick. All month, his son had been speaking of a dirt bike for the summer, coming up in a few weeks.

Nick had been doing good in school so he figured it would be well deserved and a good surprise.

"One thousand, how low do you want me to go, man? I just dropped eight hundred dollars," the Italian man shouted and threw his hands in the sky, making Moss laugh because he really was trying to give him a hard time.

"Ok, deal." Moss pulled out a wad of money.

"Damn, that's a lot of money."

"I know, thank you for your time but I'm late already so I'm placing it in my SUV right now." Moss grabbed the red and blue dirt bike.

"Wait here, get the keys," the sale guy yelled, tossing them to him.

"Thanks."

Moss knew he was behind track, so he shoved it in the back of the truck on the busy street as people shopped and walked around to enjoy the wealth.

Closing the truck, Moss felt something tell him to look over his shoulder and when he did, bullets hit his chest spinning Moss around.

BOC....

BOC....

BOC....

BOC....

The masked gunman fired four shots in Moss' head before running off down the block as civilians screamed and yelled for someone to call police.

Moss's lifeless body was now slumped on the ground, just another black man dead on the streets.

Chapter 7

Harlem, NY

A few weeks later, Moss' funeral was held at a big gravesite near Uptown and people from all over came out to pay respect and to see if the news was true. The media made Moss seem like an angel and an outstanding man with a strong character, who did so much for his community.

Those who knew Moss well did not believe a bit of it, they already knew he was a true murderer, with no soul or remorse.

Body looked around at all the unfamiliar faces after service and couldn't help but wonder why this was his first time seeing all these people. Everybody was starting to leave, except for Moss and Jalisa's real family and friends.

"Sis, I'm sorry for our loss, but I'ma kill whoever did that," Ice said, approaching in his black suit with puffy eyes. His brother's death hit him extra hard, he hadn't been able to sleep since.

"Don't make it no worse than it already is." Jalisa gave him a little hug as Ice ignored her comment.

"What's up, little Nick?" Ice saw his nephew give him a cold look.

"It's Body now and I'm fine," Body corrected him as a white man in an expensive tailor approached them.

"Good morning, my name is Mark. I was good friends with Moss, and I hear you're his wife." Mark looked at Jalisa as she thought he was some type of meat.

"Yes, I am. How may I help you, sir?"

"I'm paying my respect. Moss was family and this is for you. Once again, my apologies go out to you." Mark handed Jalisa a suitcase and walked off to a limousine.

"Mom, who is that?" Mickey, the youngest son, asked.

"I don't know," she shot back.

"Me neither, but see what's in the suitcase," said Ice being thirsty, thinking he's about to get some of whatever is in it.

"Boy, my husband just died. I'm going home with my kids." Jalisa took all three of her children and got in her Range Rover in tears, thinking who would do this to her husband.

Now she had to raise her kids alone and be a strong mother playing the mother and father role.

***

Brooklyn, NY

Six Years Later

Body waited outside a new restaurant on Flatbush Avenue for a man named Hollow, who was pushing a lot of dope and weed in the 90's section. At seventeen years old, Body had already made a name for himself, before he even graduated high school a few weeks ago.

Not too long ago after walking across stage at his high school graduation, Body's ops did a drive by, killing two teenagers on school grounds.

With so many ops at first, Body had no clue who was out to get him, but he heard it was a hit by Montay, his number one enemy of all time. Montay was from Castle Hill, right down the street from Soundview where he lived.

Two summers ago, Body robbed and killed Montay's brother and his big homie for his blood set, which started their own little war in The Bronx.

Since Moss' death, the outlook on life Body's outlook on life was, *fuck it*, and then one day he'd hear tightness, ice-cold. Body didn't get to enjoy the finer things of life as a kid, instead he robbed and killed, because of the feeling he received from it. Robbing, killing and murder for pay were all of Body's jobs. But selling drugs wasn't a part of it, instead he used to tell Top do his thing.

Top should be released today from Riker's Island after sitting up for a year fighting a first-degree murder and attempt murder charge. Top recently beat the charges and then had to sit for a ticket violation, but now was coming home.

Body made sure he copped him a fresh Dior sweatsuit with Timbs and a Dior scarf to match, because New York weather in December was frozen.

Staring out his window, Body peeped Hollow P and a sexy, dark-skinned chick come out of the food spot. It was 11:41 am. Top told Body he should be home around 2:00 pm, so Body wanted to have him something nice to match his fit.

Hollow P walked to his Benz truck with a big Cuban link hanging around his neck and a bust down Rolex watch. The snowy parking lot was empty.

"Ayo, my boy, run that," Body said as Hollow P turned around and saw a gun pointed to his face.

"Oh, my fucking God!" The female almost had a panic attack.

"Relax ma, you good... but whatever is done here stays here, right?" Body looked at the scared young lady.

"Yes," she responded, closing her eyes, already knowing how niggas gave it up when they came to collect.

"Yo cuz, you making a..." Hollow P tried to say his piece but didn't get a chance to.

BOOM....

BOOM....

BOOM....

BOOM....

Body snatched the chains and the watch off Hollow P's neck and wrist, then he ran in his pockets, taking all his money and drugs.

"You straight?" Body asked the woman, who'd just witnessed her first murder and was turned on.

"Hear no evil, see no evil," she stated, looking at Body's muscular frame and handsome dark chocolate face.

"Good, I'll see you around," Body said, running off to his hooptie. The jewelry and money were a welcome home gift to his best friend Top.

Ray was supposed to be getting shipped off to the Army this week, but he wasn't the party type, so going out tonight for Ray wasn't even a question.

***

Rikers Island Jail, NY

Hours Later

Top just got and he couldn't wait to get back to a bag but this time things, would be a little different. He used his time wisely, basically reforming his plans and coming up with new games strategies.

When he first got arrested, he thought it was over, twenty-five to life like most niggas in the jail fighting bodies. One day, Abdulla an old head, kufi wearing nigga from Harlem, pulled up on Top with a Quran already knowing he as a Blood gang member.

Abdulla gave him the Quran and walked off and Top took it upon himself to read it and became a Muslim. Top then learned his prayers in Islam they called Salat and started to pray to Allah. Then out of nowhere Top beat his case, while in the box for cutting a rival gang member named Jet Boy.

Throughout his whole bid Body and Ray, plus his girl was there for him, even when he thought it would be over because the DA wanted him to cop out to twelve years upstate.

A new all-white Challenger pulled up with tins blasting Lil Tjay's new album.

"Yuroooo…." Body shouted, rolling down and yelling out the window before climbing out the new car he bought last week and did not even tell Top about it.

"Damn boy, when you copped this, son? I can't front shit fly." Top hugged Body, happy to see him blossoming up.

"Regular Bronx shit, you heard."

"That's a fact."

"Put these on, that shit you wearing dead, gang." Body reached into the car and pulled out a Dior sweatsuit and Timbs, then surprised him with the necklace and watch he stole from Hollow P earlier today.

"Damn boy, this shit *odee* icy." Top put the chain around his neck after getting dressed in public, leaving the jail clothes on the curb.

"That's all you, bro, and the Rolex, nigga... welcome." Body then dug in his pockets to pull out a wad of blue faces and handed them over to Top, looking at the smile on his boy's face.

Nobody really knew Top caught the murder charge he beat for Body, so they would forever share that secret bond.

"Wifey at work all night tonight, and I ain't got no parole or probation, so you already know what the vibe is." Top got inside the car.

"Henny?"

"Big facts, boy. This nigga Ray still out here? I ain't hear from son in a few weeks," Top asked.

"He in training right now out there in VA, bro." Body was proud of Ray, even though he hated the Army, he was just happy to see his boy do something with his life rather than the streets.

"Oh, that's fire, but guess who blew trial two weeks ago?"

"Who?"

"Lil Eddy from Millbrook."

"Hold on. The little, short fat nigga who used to always get beat up after school?" Body remembered him clearly because he slapped Lil Eddy a few times.

"Yeah, but he is not fat no more, boy muscled up and he is running the building on big homie-style now for the Gorilla Stones," Top said, shaking his head.

"Wow, what he blew trial too? I ain't even know he was locked up. I thought son moved back to Brooklyn."

"Nah, he killed two cops in Queens two years ago and it blow trial to three life sentences."

"That's crazy." Body couldn't believe it, a nigga close to his age about to do all that time.

"The judge charged him as an adult because Lil Eddy was two years older than us. You remember his slow ass got left back twice," Top explained.

"Son was off just a little bit. I do remember that." Body laughed, gunning the car down the highway back to The Bronx, as they talked and went out to eat and get liquor.

***

Fort Lee, VA

Ray loved but hated PT, otherwise known as practice training since forever, so today it was no different. The sun was out, and he had to wear the heavy Army gear while exercising.

Today's work-out consisted of a five-mile run, a hundred burpee's, five hundred jumping jacks, four hundred squats, crunches, and two hundred regular pushupsfor the males. The females had to do the same thing, but the rep amount was cut in half.

Coming to the Army was the best thing that could happen to Ray because the streets was calling his name, the gangs, drugs, and violence.

Seeing his best friend Top catch a murder case tightened him right up and made him change his life, now he was in the Army, trying to get his life in order. Now with a new career ahead of him, he felt productive and as if he could achieve more things in life.

Chapter 8

Manhattan, NY

Jalisa looked just as beautiful as she did six years ago when her husband passed away. Moss' loss was a hard pill to swallow, but as a mother and strong woman, she had to take control over her emotions and hold shit down.

Everything's been good for Jalisa, her daughter was in college at Pace University in Westchester County. Mickey the youngest was now in high school, and Body she hated to even thing about at times because of the path he was going down.

A few weeks ago, Jalisa found six guns in his room. She made him get them all outta there and cursed Body out, almost about to kick him out she was so mad.

Whenever she looked at Body, her late husband popped up in her head because they looked alike and now Body was following his footsteps. She knew he'd been in the streets since high school but for some reason, Jalisa didn't think he sold drugs, it had to be something else.

Today's been a busy at work but luckily, it's almost over, her feet ached from wearing Gucci heels all day.

"Jalisa!" an older white woman yelled, coming downstairs.

"Yes, Nicole?"

"The higher-ups want to see you upstairs," Nicole said, outta breath.

"Me?"

"Yes, you."

"For what?" Jalisa got a little nervous, wondering what she did wrong because this job was important to her. It was her life, not to mention it fed her family.

"Their waiting on you."

"Alright." Jalisa followed her upstairs, thinking about the recent employees that got fired, which left Jalisa the only black woman working in the bank.

Once upstairs, Jalisa's heart was beating at a rapid pace, all types of bad thoughts flooded her brain. Nicole opened the French cherry wood double doors that led to three white men sitting at a round table, laughing and smoking cigars.

Jalisa knew one of the men as Mr. Watts, the bank manager and another one of them she saw stop by a few times.

"Good afternoon, Jalisa," Mr. Watts stated.

"Hey." Jalisa didn't really know what to say.

"Nicole, you can leave now. Thank you, darling, for your time." Mr. Watts looked at Nicole as she shook her head and walked out, hoping Jalisa got fired because she disliked the best workers in the bank for stealing her shine.

"Jalisa, nice to meet you. Have a seat, my name is Mr. Sims. You know Mr. Watts, and this is Mr. Mark," greeted Mr. Sims, smiling.

"How's everybody doing today?" Jalisa asked, sitting down and looking at Mr. Mark, trying to see where she knew him from.

"You look a little nervous, are you?" Mr. Watts asked her.

"Only a little," she replied.

"No need to be, Jalisa. I'm the CEO of the company and I've been watching your work ethic, as I told Mr. Watts. I recently bought the whole bank from him two years ago, but I'd already had a big piece of it for ten years now. Anyway, I want to promote you to bank manager and raise your pay. I want you to control the other two locations, because Nicole will no longer be with us after today. She stole from me all these years and blamed it on the blacks," Mr. Mark said.

Jalisa couldn't believe what she was hearing. Her body felt glued to the chair and her mouth felt glued shut also.

"No need to respond, we know you gladly accept," Mr. Sims laughed at his own comment seeing Jalisa's shocked expression.

"Yes, thank you. I'm very appreciative for this moment." Jalisa's words were short but honest.

"No problem, you deserve it," Mr. Mark said before Jalisa got up to leave, pulling down her skirt that hugged her nice ass.

"What happened when they fired you?" Nicole rushed her.

"Nothing."

"Huh? Now that's weird." Nicole had a real confused look on her face are like she's hoping for it.

"I'm the new manager of all the banks," Jalisa bragged with a smile, just to rub it in her face as two NYPD cops came upstairs.

"A black person, what?" Nicole was now pissed off.

"Nicole, you're fired! And going to jail for stealing eighteen million of the company's funds. Officers," Mr. Watts said as the police placed Nicole in handcuffs, taking her away as she screamed things out about their secret affair.

Mr. Watts was also getting tired of Nicole calling his home starting trouble with his wife, so everything worked out just fine.

"Thanks again, Mr. Mark, and where do I know you from, if you don't mind me asking?" Jalisa couldn't match Mark's face yet, but he looked so familiar.

"Your husband was a good friend of mine, a while back," Mr. Mack replied.

"That's right, you came out to the funeral and gave me the money," she recalled.

"Yes, that was me. how is the family?"

"Good, no complaints."

"Nice. Well, I have to get going, enjoy your new position," Mr. Mark told her before walking off.

"I will, thank you." Jalisa really was amazed at how God works because she was about to ask Nicole for some extra hours to get in overtime, and now she's the boss.

***

Spanish Harlem, NY

Papa hated waiting on people, especially people who worked for him, it made Papa feel like the worker. Papa is one of the biggest suppliers in the city and his name was very powerful and strong.

Sitting in the back of a Bentley truck, his two guards saw the headlights of a Porsche pull up in front of them.

"He's here," one of the goons told Papa.

"Wait here for me," Papa said, slowly getting out the back with a cane because he'd just had knee surgery two days ago.

It'd just stopped raining an hour ago, so it was still a little wet outside as Papa walked up to Magic, one of his main clients from The Bronx area, moving a lot of weight.

"Sorry I'm late, boss, traffic was a little crazy over here," Magic said, seeing Papa's face wasn't so friendly.

"Do I look like your bitch?"

"No never, it was a mistake," Magic stated again, knowing how crazy the little man could get at times.

"Make sure it won't happen again. Next time, I won't be so nice. Now come on, so we can get this shit over with. I hate being out here," Papa said, looking around a Catholic church parking lot.

Magic went to his trunk and grabbed two heavy duffle bags full of money. "This is everything right here."

"Ok, I'll have my nephew call you with all the details later on today," Papa said as he walked off.

"Iight." Magic climbed in his car, thinking about the load he had coming. Working for a kingpin like Papa made Magic very rich.

Chapter 9

South Bronx

Steel walked back and forth in one of his traps he used to only break down keys and bag up any product he got from Ice.

Having a cousin like Ice in his corner couldn't have been better because not too long ago, Steel was a trigger-happy little nigga running around The Bronx and Harlem booking low level local drug dealers.

The long scar he got across his face came from a bitch during a robbery in Harlem. She snuck up on Steel from behind and cut his face wide open, giving her man time to get ahold of his weapon as Steel had a BB gun that day. Steel took off, running zig-zag shooting from his lick he didn't get shit off of.

Today, Ice was coming with the work and Steel had been dry for three days, so his crew and personal clients were going crazy.

Getting money and spending paper is what Steel lived by, he loved to show off and stunt when his crew went out to clubs or even in the hood.

Growing up in Harlem and The Bronx, he lived all over the city, even with some Long Island niggas he did a bid with in his prime early teens upstate.

The apartment buzzer rang, and he rushed to the door to let Ice inside then unlock the chains on the door. Steel got overly excited and started talking to himself as the door opened.

"Yurooo…." Steel embraced Ice and saw no duffle bag. Ice always came with the drugs in a bag.

"What's the vibes, boy? It stank in this bitch you smoking that shit again," Ice referred to Steel smoking PCP.

"Nah bro, I ain't fuck with that shit since I beat up police, but where is the work at, son?" Steel asked, closing the door, but Pasco entered with a big travel Under Armor bag.

"Right there." Ice pointed at Pasco, who was a Harlem nigga and Steel hated him over his ex-bitch but when Pasco started moving drugs for Ice in Harlem, he had no choice but to be cool and mature.

"Oh iight," Steel's words were very short as he walked into the kitchen to see what Ice's plan was for the shipment.

"Let's sort this hit out, we got the keys right here." Ice took the duffle bag from Pasco and opened it, pouring it all over the kitchen counter.

"Thirty-five? Damn, we bout to touch and triple this shit, my little niggas up there litty," Pasco stated.

"I'ma put five to the side for Afro, he about to be home from up top next week." Ice put five keys near him for his best friend, who just did a decade in New York State Prison for a murder.

"My traps doing numbers, so I need more than ten," Pasco said, already putting the math together in his head.

"I got chu," Ice replied, seeing Steel's face frown because he needed at least ten joints.

Ice took ten for himself and gave Steel five birds, then handed fifteen to Pasco whose face lit up like a Christmas tree.

"Good looks, boy. You know I'm getting right to it, regular Harlem shit." Pasco looked over at Steel's face and gave off a light grin.

"Pasco, before you take that, I got a question." Ice caught him off guard.

"What's the word, Ice?" Pasco responded by still fighting with Steel.

"You ever tatted on a nigga?" asked Ice.

"Who me? Fuck nah, son. On gang, I never stacked on no nigga, bro. What you getting at, Ice?" Sweat popped up on Pasco's bald head for the first time in a while.

"When you was eighteen years old in White Plains Federal Court, you pointed out the man who killed your sister, and sold your uncle seven kilos of dope," Ice spoke with a certain sign and Steel was more shocked than anything because he never heard dirt on Pasco's name before.

"Come on, Ice. I was young," Pasco gave in, not trying to hide it.

"Nigga, that happened two years ago. Are you still working for them people?" Ice asked, pulling out a pistol.

"No, I said that only one time. They made me do it, bro. I'm not a rat." Pasco tried to justify his wrongdoing.

"Damn boy, you were or are the whole time." Steel laughed in shock.

"I know how to get money." Pasco saw Ice lift his weapon and did a silent prayer.

BOC....

BOC....

BOC....

BOC....

BOC....

BOC....

Blood squirted on a few keys before Pasco's body flipped out the chair onto the floor.

"Them blocks he used to have in Harlem, I want you and Montay to run them shits now. Take all thirty keys and give half to Montay, you heard?" said Ivy, before leaving the apartment.

Steel had to clean the blood up and get rid of Pasco, which had to be done at night because people in the area watched the building closely and they most likely had heard the gunshots.

***

Ice drove to his girl's house in Mount Vernon and spent some time with her, but their fun time consisted of sex.

"Ohhhh shittt, daddy..." Kard moaned as Ice pulled on the fake hair from behind, hitting her phat ass doggystyle.

Kard was a short Jamaican bitch with a big ass and cute face, but the only thing wrong with her was the way her teeth lined up.

"You love this pussy, fuck me hard," she screamed as if her kids weren't in the next room trying to sleep.

"Hmmmm, I'm bout to cum, bitch." Ice pulled her ass cheeks apart and went deeper, sticking his thumb in her brown hole making her squirt, until he came. They fucked forty more minutes, then Ice had to go handle some business.

Chapter 10

Soundview, The Bronx

Body put on one of his fly outfits, about to attend a night basketball game near Cortlandt Projects. The night game over there be litty, everybody be in there, plus all the beautiful women would come out to the gym where it went down at.

Every year when the weather got nice outside, basketball games would be hosted all over The Bronx and Washington Heights. The best of the best usually came to play ball in June, July and August.

There was a knock at the door, and he put this gun in the top dresser drawer.

"Come in, yo," he yelled to whoever was playing games, standing on the other side.

"What are you doing?" Mickey asked, walking inside with his little bop, showing off his new Jordans he got from their mom.

"But to slide out, little nigga, what's the vibes."

"Nothing, about to go see a movie with my friends." Mickey had friends for days.

"You need some paper?" Body pulled out two hundred dollars off a wad of money.

"Thanks, bro."

"You good, son."

"Mommy was looking for you earlier, but I didn't see you," said Mickey, about to walk out so he could meet his friends.

"How did she look?"

"Regular. I don't know when she mad or happy, it's always the same face to me," Mickey told him before walking out.

"Damn," Body mumbled leaving his room, but he took his gun and car keys.

Jalisa's room wasn't too far from the bathroom, so he knocked on the door only to hear the TV, until he knocked once more.

"Body, that you?" Jalisa yelled.

"Yes, Mom." He walked inside to see her laying down watching *Chicago PD*, as she did every weekend on her free time.

"I came looking for you earlier," she guzzled looking at his expensive Louis Vuitton fit.

"Sorry, I was out with Top."

"He's home?" Jalisa wasn't too happy because she thought Top was a bad influence on Body since they were kids.

"Yeah, he's chillin and looking for a job," Body lied.

"I bet he is." Jalisa shook her head, already smelling the lies.

"How's work anyway? I barely see you, Mom."

"That's because you're never here, and your sister told me to tell you about a party at her school she wants you to go to next week."

"How's Brooklyn doing in school?" Body asked, already knowing she was very smart and a forever honor roll student since the second grade.

"Your sister is as you young kids say nowadays, litty."

"Mom… don't say that, you don't even sound right," he joked, sitting on her bed.

"So, picture how you sound, and I may be getting old, but I look better than a lot of young women in your age bracket." She spoke the truth, so he just nodded his head.

Since he was a kid, everywhere they went dudes always tried to holla at her, but she never gave them a chance.

"Facts."

"That's your car?"

"What car?" Body played dumb.

"Let's not do that, son." Jalisa gave him an honest look.

"Yes."

"Park that shit down the block and don't ever let me find another gun in here. I have a younger son who is blind to that lifestyle, you understand?" She looked at her son and saw Moss all in his face, even when he did the stupid look.

"Ok, I got you, Mom."

"Good, now let me enjoy my show. I'll see you later," she told him, knowing he was about to go out somewhere.

"Love you."

"Love you too, my son," Jalisa said as Body then walked out.

***

Thirty Minutes Later

When all the kids left the house, and it got peaceful and quiet, Jalisa hopped up outta bed and quickly got dressed. Jalisa had a secret life not too many knew about besides the people she had dealings with.

Six years prior, after Moss' death, Jalisa found a lot of kilos of coke and started to make big moves in Brooklyn with a few cousins she knew from there. Jalisa lowkey became one of the biggest dealers in Brooklyn.

She got herself together and left in her BMW truck, on the expressway headed to Brooklyn for a meeting with her top soldier.

The whole ride there, all she could think about was her sons, praying the crazy streets didn't touch their souls as it took her within six years.

Jalisa never thought she would be selling drugs at a queen pin level, and her connection was in Miami. She wanted to keep her business as far away from The Bronx as possible, because New York niggas be hating hard, especially when a bitch is supplying a whole damn borough.

Landing in Brooklyn, the meetup spot was in Red Hook, an area her cousin Rock-O grew up in and had on lock. She pulled up near Red Hook Projects, and Rock-O was awaiting her as he got inside her truck.

Rock-O spend twenty minutes telling her about the next drug order and money transactions. He also told Jalisa about how Hollow P, one of his main workers, was recently robbed and killed in broad daylight. But she didn't give two fucks, she wanted her money, that was how she operated.

Romell Tukes

Chapter 11

Hunts Point, The Bronx

Montay left one of his Spanish bitch's crib on Fox Lane. He'd been fucking her all day long and she wanted him to stay, but it was Friday night.

On Friday nights, his traps normally saw the most profits in The Bronx and Harlem. Growing up in the Castle Hill section of the city, all he knew was how to get money, him and his tower brothers who ran Castle Hill Projects.

A while back, one of his brothers was murdered by a member of Body's crew and since then, it's been a crazy war. Soundview niggas wasn't allowed in Castle Hill and vice versa, shit turned into little Iraq.

Montay was only a few years older than Body, but he still considered him a little nigga, even though Montay knew of his outstanding body count.

Trying to focus on money and the ongoing drama turned into a job itself, but he understood what all came with the game, good and bad times.

Driving to Castle Hill, he saw his little cousin dressed like a hooker, with a group of young girls no older than sixteen.

"Jenny, get your ass over here." Montay couldn't believe she's in the cold with heels and a skirt on.

"Hey Montay," Jenny said with her strong Spanish accent.

"Why did you dress like that?'' he asked as she sucked her teeth.

"We're going to a party, it's Friday. My mom knows," she replied, leaning into the Range Rover as her friends eyed Montay, wondering who wanted to get a ride. Montay was Dominican and Black, with a nice tanned-skin complexion, waves and a handsome face.

"Iight, your little ass better not be out here thotting."

"Montay, come on, this not even me."

"That's what they all say… but call me if you need something."

"Bye," she shot back rudely as he pulled off into traffic.

Montay got a call from a chick in Harlem, but he ignored it, seeing NYPD park on the corner. Getting pulled over was not in his plans at all, especially with a hundred grand in cash and two fully loaded handguns in the back.

***

Soundview, The Bronx

Top woke up, looking over to his clock thinking about what the fuck he was gonna do today, because the winter was starting to break so Top wanted to get out.

Checking his pants pockets, he saw the wad of money left from what Body gave him last week.

"Shopping," Top told himself looking at his iPhone seeing a gang of missed calls.

He still had his chick TiTi's car parked out front, so he didn't need a ride, but called Body to see if his boy wanted to roll to Bay Plaza with him.

"Top of the morning, my guy," Body answered as if he is already up and moving around in his crib.

"What are you doing, bro? I caught up at the wrong time?" Top asked, hearing heavy breathing and puffs.

"Nah, I'm exercising. Gotta get my shit back right for the summer, word to mother," Body said, while doing push-ups.

"Fuck all dat shit, bro. I did all that shit on the Island every day, but I'm about to pull up."

"Iight, I'm here, what are you trying to do?" Body knew Top wanted to go somewhere or do something.

"I wanna go pick up some outfits, bro. You saw how nice it is outside?" Top asked, looking out his own bedroom window.

"Facts, I'm down. Let me hop in the shower real quick, bro"

"Say that. I'ma do the same,'' Top shot back, hanging up going to the shower, glad his sister and mom was at work.

***

An Hour Later

Top pulled up to Body's crib playing loud music, a new song from one of his favorite rappers, 22 G'z outta Brooklyn drill music scene.

Waiting for Body to come out seemed like forever but Top didn't see the shadow that appeared at his window.

"What the fuck, little nigga? You almost scared the shit outta me," Top shouted to Mickey, seeing him smile. "You just lucky I ain't shoot your little black bad ass."

"You ain't shooting shit," Mickey said, running in the house as Body finally came out.

"That little nigga supposed to be in school," Body said, climbing in the car wondering who his boy stole it from.

"He's bad as hell, I swear." Top shook his head pulling off.

"I forgot to tell you about this upcoming weekend," Body said as Top reached for a blunt in the arm rest.

"Where?"

"Pace University, bro."

"What the fuck is that?" Top acted as if the name was foreign.

"Brooklyn goes there. It's in Westchester, she want a nigga to pull up, son."

"Ok, we in there, son. Now I can get an outfit for that shit"

"Word. I know she got the bitches." Body knew his sister had wild friends, but she never let him get close to them.

"How long she been in college?"

"Brooklyn got one or two years left, bro. She about to be litty, doing the CSI crime shit. I forgot the name of it."

"Forensics Science shit."

"Facts. I'm proud of sis," Body said as they talked and chilled all day at the mall, bagging chicks.

Romell Tukes

Chapter 12

Westchester County, NY

Pace University ranked in the top five colleges in New York state. The campus was big, with all types of students from all over the world. Body wasn't heavy into partying, but he hadn't seen Brooklyn in months, so he figured tonight would be the best time to surprise her.

"Yo, you think Brooklyn still likes me?" Top asked in the passenger seat drinking a nutcracker, which was liquor and juice mixed.

"Nigga, she never liked you." Body's remark did not sit to well with him. Since they were kids, everybody knew how much Top had a crush on Brooklyn. But she always dubbed him when he tried to ask her out.

"You just saying that because she is your sister."

"Never that. I'm not a hater, bro, but if a bitch don't like you, I won't sugar coat it. Plus, you not on the level Brooklyn is on some real independent black powerful woman shit" Body admired his sister's style and class, but he felt sad fo many nigga she dated, if they could not keep up with her.

"This shit packed." Top changed the subject, seeing how the parking lot barely had space for them to park.

"Word boy, I think her dorm is right over there," Body said, parking besides a Jeep that looked familiar.

"I'm trying to fuck something in this bitch," Top said, seeing thick white chicks walk through the parking area.

"Shit... I agree, bro, so you might gotta leave in an Uber," Body joked but if the situation did come into play, then Top already knew what he would have to do.

Both of them rocked black owned sweatsuits with Yeezy sneakers to match their drip.

"Damn son, I shoulda came to college, gangsta," Top said out loud looking at all the beautiful women from different races.

"It's never too late."

"They would kick me out this bitch because my first day, I'm flooding the school with drugs bro, on gang." Top knew colleges were a gold mine, but the only thing was not getting snitched on.

"You buggin."

"Picture how many of these rich white kids sniff coke, do dope," Top said as they reached the Brooklyn building.

"Most of these kids' parents are lawyers, judges and federal law agents, fuck with them if you want." Body heard loud music from his sister's complex saw people outside smoking and drinking have a good time.

Walking into the dimmed apartment, loud rap music blasted and weed smoke could be smelled in the air, bitches as dancing all over the place like they were in a strip club.

"Yoo, this shit popping, look at the Spanish chick doing a split on the countertop about to bust her ass," Top pointed out.

"She wildin."

"Brother!" a loud voice shouted over the music.

"Brooklyn, what's the vibe?" Top tried to cut her off from giving Body a hug, because she was looking good in a green and white dress with heels.

"Boy, move!" Brooklyn pushed Top out the way and jumped in Body's arms.

"Where is the rest of your clothes?" Body asked, seeing she had titties and ass out all over the place.

Brooklyn had dark, long and thick, jet-black hair, smooth skin, juicy lips, and was very beautiful. Most men begged for her attention.

"My clothes in the dresser. Relax it's a party not a wedding, bro. But I'm glad you pulled up," she said, smelling must coming from one of the females dancing on the wall with a football player.

"I had to come out and I missed you."

"No, you didn't." She knew Body was lying because he would have called to check on her.

"Facts. I been odee busy," Body said as he looked to his left and saw a familiar face that left him stuck. Brooklyn peeped at who he couldn't stop staring at, then realized what was going on.

"You ain't know she went to school here?" asked Brooklyn.

"Nah I thought she moved or went to the Army. That was the last thing I heard about her," said Body, who still watched his middle school and high school crush, chill with her friends in a corner.

"She single, really smart, and a boss bitch like me, but wait here she come. I'm out." Brooklyn dipped off.

Body saw Hope coming and got nervous. He looked around for Top, but he was nowhere to be found. A new song from Yung Blue came on, which lightened the room and slowed down the tempo.

"In my heart I know that was you, but my better judgment thought against it," Hope said loud enough just so he could hear her.

"You look nice," was all he could say.

"Thank you. What are you doing here, partying was never your thing."

"Brooklyn lives here."

"Oh yeah, I forgot Brooklyn is your sister. How could I forget?" Hope felt dumb.

"I thought you went to the Army?"

"That was just a rumor. I wanted to try college would open up more doors and opportunities for me."

"That's real, I guess. I saw your Jeep outside, but when I tried to match the face, I couldn't," Body admitted.

"I love my Jeep, but what you been up to?"

"Living life." Body tried to cut it short because telling Hope his real-life events would be a big turn off.

"Oh ok, I see. It's loud in there, let's go outside." Hope grabbed his hand, leading him outside so they could talk. Hope was one of the prettiest chicks in the school. She was all natural, light brown and slim-thick, perfect smile, with chinky brown eyes. Her attitude was the most special thing about her. They talked for two hours and ended up going out to eat at a local diner, leaving Top behind.

Romell Tukes

Chapter 13

Brooklyn, East New York

Days Later

Body wanted to bring Top along with him, but his boy been laid up with the same bad Spanish chick he met at Pace University this past weekend, she was from Miami. The same night he chilled with Hope at the diner, Top was smashing the little Spanish bitch.

Tonight, he was on a mission, scoping out a nigga he been hearing about for months now getting to a bag all over East New York. Doing dirt in The Bronx wasn't smart in his book so he did jobs in Brooklyn, Harlem, Queens, Manhattan, Long Island, Staten Island, and he took jobs in Westchester. The only way Body would take a job in The Bronx is if it was big time.

A nigga named Woody T put him on to Teddy and his crew so now Buddy wasn't letting. Body had the drop on Teddy as he followed him all through the East in an older Honda Accord.

There hasn't been a day that's passed since he saw Hope that she wouldn't pop up in his head daily, but Body knew she was a good girl who had lived a hard life, because her brother and dad had been murdered in the streets.

When Hope expressed this to Body, he informed her he recently landed a job at Home Depot. He lied, and she jacked it. That night he tried to do everything to prove to her he was different, but when reality kicked in, Body felt like he was the same nigga Hope spoke down about and disliked.

Hope asked if he was speaking to any other females at the time and not trying to be full of lies, he told her yes but nothing serious and she respected that. The two planned to go out on a date in a few days to City Island, nothing special.

Body made a left down a street, passing Bama Projects, a well-known area for violence and drug trafficking. Not trying to play Teddy too close, he parked at the end of the block, watching Teddy get out his car to dap up some dark ugly nigga who had a laundry bag.

The only thing that ran through Body's mind was what was in the bag, because it looked heavy and filled with more than clothes.

Teddy looked at his cousin Jo and then the laundry bag, shaking his head trying to make sense of everything.

"They're gonna run down tonight at midnight and before they hit us, I want you to take it," Jo stated, carrying the bag to Teddy's trunk.

"Fuck son, y'all bugging how come you ain't bring this to Hassan?" Teddy asked, looking around nervously as Jo put the drugs in his Cadillac.

"Out in Atlanta with P Roc and Gutta."

"Where do I put this shit at, bro?"

"It's yours, I don't know but I think I got somebody a few blocks away. We can leave it at their crib," said Jo, thinking of his ex-boyfriend's mom.

"Yeah, because if the block is hot, niggas gonna know it was my shit and we can't take no more losses, or Rock-O gonna kill both of us," Teddy stated seriously.

"Bro, I ain't going shit to do with that crazy nigga. You give me the drugs and I sell it, nigga. You give me the drugs and I sell it son." Jo didn't want no problems at all when it came to Rock-O nobody did.

"Come on, so you can drop this shit off." Teddy looked at his watch before getting in the car and pulling off, unaware of the Honda on his rear end lurking.

Less than four minutes later, Teddy and Jo arrived at their designation on a side block, which was dark and quiet.

"Let me call her first," Jo said as he pulled out a cell phone.

"You shoulda been did that, dumb ass nigga." Teddy hated his cousin slow ways of thinking.

"I forgot, gang, chill the fuck out. You know I be high as shit."

"Man, just call the bitch," Teddy shouted getting impatient.

"Iight, son." When Jo dialed the number, he felt a gun pressed to his head.

"Any of you bitches move, I'll turn these tan seats into red leather," Body said, barefaced looking at both men in his kill zone.

"Bruh, before you do this shit, just know we work for Rock-O and if you from Brooklyn, then you know he is coming," Teddy said before Body fired four bullets into Jo's head, scaring the shit outta Teddy.

"Fuck Rocky or Rock-O, nigga, pop the trunk and go slow." Body had his head in the passenger window aiming his gun directly at Teddy.

"Ok, bro." Teddy slowly did as he was told and popped the trunk.

"Good boy."

"I'm straight?" Teddy asked, looking at Body out the side of his eye.

"Facts."

Boc....

Boc....

Body got the laundry bag out the trunk, jumped back into his Honda his homegirl let him use and got ghost.

Forty minutes later, he met up with Top in the Uptown section of The Bronx and had a big smile on his face. Top climbed outta a BMW Sedan.

"You're doing big things, fresh homie, cuffing pussy," Body said.

"Nah, shawty a vibe and her people got a bag."

"Fuck her bag, you about to get rich, take that laundry bag right here." Body pointed to the back.

"What the fuck, bro? This is kilos and money."

"I know, fifty-fifty, bro. I know you hustle so do what you do but have mines" Body said with a chuckle while top lock through the big bag.

"Say dat. I'm bout to put shit in motion tonight. Love you, boy." Top gave Body a pound and took the drugs and money, plotting his next move in his head because he was about to get rich.

Romell Tukes

Chapter 14

Westside, The Bronx

Top counted everything last night at his crib and couldn't believe what it all came out to. There were twenty bricks of white coke, ten pounds of exotic weed, and eighteen thousand in cash.

First thing he planned to do was cop a new car, after he paid his cousin Gage a visit to drop him off some drugs in the Burnside section. All night Top brainstormed about who he could trust with the drugs and to bring his cut back because the Bronx niggas were all mostly cutthroat.

Texting while driving, his new little chick Paula was blowing his phone up, but Top loved it and shawty had it hard for him already.

"Hey baby." Top put the call on the speaker, pushing the BMW through traffic.

"I miss you," Paula replied with a sweet voice.

"Miss you too, how's school?

"I'm about to go back to my dorm and study until you get here. Where are you anyway?" She threw it out there.

"Driving."

"Where to?"

"In The Bronx to see my cousin real quick, then I'ma cop me a car."

"Why get a car and you can use mines?" she questioned.

"I know you got shit to do, baby."

"Not really, I coulda bought you a car today, baby... a Benz, BMW, Porsche or Wraith. Whatever you wanted," Paula shot back letting him know when money was long.

"Thanks boo, but I'm good for now. I'm not broke, you just met me at a bad time," he explained.

"You're not cheating on me, are you?" she asked outta nowhere.

"Baby, I don't got time to cheat," Top shot back, seeing red flags because they weren't even together yet.

"Ok. I believe you, papi, and you left your gun here. I'ma become a cop next year, baby, so you have to be more cautious around me with weapons."

"Oh yeah, I forgot my baby about to be a federal agent." He remembered her telling him this the first night they fucked even though he was drunk.

"Yep, well call me when you're on your way and I'm horny, so I want some dick all down my throat," Paula's voice got extra sexy.

"No doubt, ma. I'm give you all dat and some."

"Can't wait," Paula said, before hanging up

Top pulled up to his cousin's block, thinking about Paula's head game. It was ok but he needed it to be better, so he made a mental note to teach her how to deep throat and go crazy on the dick.

Gage posted up outside when Top pulled up. It was a cool day, so everybody rocked sweat suits, even Top.

"What's up, cuz? Welcome homie, I heard you beat that man down," Gage said sticking his head in the window.

"Nigga, get in." Tags always talked to his cousin like a bitch nigga because he was, but Gage knew how to get money.

"This shit fly, peanut butter seats and all that," Gage said, sinking in the seats.

"I got a position for you."

"Listen, I'm not killing nobody. I hear about you and Body don't forget I also fed up with y'all."

"Nigga, shut up, this is your lane," Top said.

"Work?" Gage sounded shocked.

"Yeah, goofy. I got coke and weed for you, but I want seventy-five percent off everything."

"Damn, you raping me, bro. Shit real out here, my nigga, talk nice." Gage sold grams and it was all his profit but he loved extra money.

"Ok, seventy percent that's it."

"Bet, how many grams is it?" Asked Gage

"It's ten keys of coke and ten pounds of weed."

"What are you serious about?" Gage's eyes widened.

"Yeah, it's too much for you, so I'll go to Motto or Michel PJ's to see lite and shorts," Top stated, pushing the start button that started the car.

"Nah, I got it, bro. I get money."

"Iight cool, take this and call me when you done, bro." Top handed his cousin a little kid bookbag.

"Say less, give me a few days."

"Gage, don't play with my paper, I don't give a fuck if we cousins."

"Top, I love my life and kids." Gage gave him a sincere look, letting Top knew he was in good hands.

"Bet, hit me." Top then pulled off, going to a car dealer to ship in New Jersey to cop a nice whip.

***

Harlem, NY

"Mommy, how old is Grandma today?" Mickey asked in the backseat of the truck as they arrived at Ms. Dee's brownstone in a nice Harlem area.

"Never ask a woman her age," Jalisa replied, taking a look at Body on his phone, letting him know to put it away because Granny didn't like cell phones in her house.

"Why?" Mickey questioned.

"Boy, shut up and stop asking dumb shit," Body spoke up.

"Watch your mouth and come on, it's your grandma's birthday, everybody play nice," Jalisa told them knowing her mom could be a handful.

Their grandma lived on the first floor and Jalisa had a key to her mom's crib. Walking in, the smell of good food filled the air, Ms. Dee was from down south so she could cook her ass off.

"Is that my baby and grandbabies?" Ms. Dee said in the kitchen.

"Yes Mom, happy birthday."

"Happy Birthday," Body and Mickey both said at the same time.

"Everybody came by. Thank you, baby, but where is the other little boy?" Ms. Dee asked, knowing someone was missing.

"Mom, that's Hope and she is a girl." Jalisa shook her head, knowing Ms. Dee meant no harm she was just getting a little old.

"Oops, I haven't been wearing my glasses lately," Ms. Dee said, seeing Mickey with a cell phone in his hand and her facial expression changed as her eyes zoomed in on him.

"You ok, Grandma?" Mickey asked, forgetting her pet peeve about cell phones.

Back in the day, Ms. Dee was married to one of the biggest dope boys in the south, until he got locked up by the feds because his brother and uncle ratted on him. Ms. Dee got arrested also on a murder charge, but her boyfriend took the charge so she could go free. The feds had all types of wire taps on phones, so since then she disliked being around phones on or off the feds could still listen to conversations.

"Get that fucking phone out my house!" Ms. Dee yelled, about to get turned up.

"Mickey, go put it in the car like I told you, hardheaded boy." Jalisa grabbed him and sent him outside.

Body went in the living room to see old pictures of his mom and couldn't believe how bad she used to be but still is. The rest of the day was cool. They spent the day with Ms. Dee as she smoked four blunts of weed and went to sleep.

Chapter 15

Flatbush, Brooklyn

Rock-O didn't look so happy as he talked to his boy Waters about the situation that happened with Teddy.

"So, I just got lost?" Rock-O asked Waters, who was his Capo and control of the reinforcement team although out Brooklyn.

"Yeah son, niggas got caught lacking, boy. Gangsta, I'm mad about that," Waters stated, leaning on Rock-O's car.

"Where it happen at?"

"East New York. That's the crazy part, them niggas got caught out in their own hood, but I think it's more to it because the hitters went straight for the work." Waters had been trying to do the math since Teddy's death hit the streets.

"You think them Pink House niggas did it?" asked Rock-O, trying to figure it out.

"Nah B, because Smooth the one who told me about it and he turned that shit boy, facts of life."

"Shit boy, what happened to Flames from the Villie? I know him and Teddy had serious beef out here." Rock-O knew how sneaky and deadly Flames was, because he did a bid with him upstate years ago.

"Flames got locked up for a murder last week in Yonkers," Waters told him, watching a NYPD van drive by slowly, already knowing who the big-time drug dealer was.

"I'ma figure it out but let me go give me a few days to take care of this and get you back loopy."

"Facts. Say that, big bro," Water replied, embarrassing his childhood friend leaving.

Rock sat in his car for a second, thinking how he was gonna explain this shit to his plug J Baby, which is Jalisa's street name. Rocko had enough money to replace the shit, but he still wanted to let her know what was going on.

***

Cortland, The Bronx

Weeks Later

Top's cousin invited him to a cookout because springtime was approaching, and the city was about to be lit again. Top had a lot of family in The Bronx all over, some he didn't even know or deal with.

"Bro, this shit fake packed," Body said leaned back in Top's Audi A8 he recently brought a few weeks ago.

"I see. I'ma bag me something nice." Top rode through Cortlandt Park looking at all the fly Spanish mamis and black chicks.

"Paula gonna whip your ass," Body joked but he was serious, because Paula has been acting crazy lately on Top. He told Body everything.

"Man, ole girl be tripping, bro. I'ma have to cut her loose soon"

"I told you about fucking with bitches' hearts and fucking them too good," Body laughed.

"Watch, Hope gonna start tripping on you soon too." Top pulled into the parking spot.

"Never boy, my bop too different." Body saw a lot of beautiful women entering and leaving the park.

"I ain't see Natural's sexy ass since school, bro. This her going away cook-out," Tap informed Body, making their way towards the cookout filled with teens and few adults.

"That's your cousin, right?"

"Yeah, so what? I'll still hit." Top saw the look Body gave him, but he didn't care. Natural was one of the baddest redbones he'd ever seen. She was thick, with green eyes, dimples, and a sexy smile.

"Nasty ass," Body said, walking through a crowd of people.

"Yo, what the fuck," Top said, not watching where he was walking and almost ran over Natural and a group of girls she was talking to.

Natural's ass looked so phat in her leggings Top couldn't help but stare for a second.

"Cuzzy, you came," Natural said, giving Top a hug.

"I had to pull up, you're gonna go to college in Texas, right?" Top responded.

"No, you ass, in Alabama," she replied, punching him in his shoulder.

"Well, hey Body!" Hope spoke out from the sideline, but nobody saw her, not even Body.

'Oh, shit. I didn't see you." Body gave her a hug, cutting right between the other women.

"Damn, hi to you also," Natural said with an attitude, wondering how Body and the girl Hope got so close, because she always had a crush on him.

Before Body could respond, he saw Montay lifting a gun from few feet away.

"Duck!" Body yelled. He started pushing the women down as shots rang out.

BLOC....

BLOC....

BLOC....

BLOC....

BLOC....

Body and Top both reacted by firing back, hitting one of Montay's people, while two innocent teens also got hit with stray bullets. The gun battle lasted a couple more seconds before the two crews ran off, with the chaos leaving three people dead at the scene and one of them was Natural.

Romell Tukes

Chapter 16

Burnside, The Bronx

Early this morning, Top got a call from Gage, telling him to pull up ASAP to his mom's crib. At first, Top thought it was something bad until Gage told him everything was good.

The park shooting two days ago had been all over the news, and Top kinda felt it's his fault Natural wasn't here anymore, even though Montay's bullet took her out.

Body decided to lay low, but Top had money to make in the streets and luckily for them, police had no leads at all on the case, so he felt like he got away with murder literally.

Gage saw Top pulling up and jumped off the stoop with a big smile.

"What popping, bro? It's ten in the morning, I hope you got some important shit to tell me."

"Facts. Come upstairs, bro." Gage walked in the building, taking the stairs to the third floor.

"Where are you, Mom?"

"She drive school buses, nigga, but I'm about to get my own spot in a couple of days, because she about to be litty." Gage opened the front door to his mom's crib and went straight to the back room.

Walking into Gage's bedroom, Top couldn't believe all the money he saw in piles, neatly stacked in rubber bands.

"This is crazy, my boy, you made all that?" Top pointed at the money smiling and glad he woke up for this.

"Hell yeah, the way my fiends cooked that shit up had people going crazy son" Gage admitted.

"Oh word, so the product was hitting like that, B?"

"Word to my dead, bro."

"Bag all that shit up and I'm coming by a little later to scoop it." Top turned to leave.

'You gonna get more, right?" Gage eyes opened extremely wide as if he was getting high.

"Give me until later," Top promised.

"Ok, bet. Bro, shit litty out here, crackheads coming from all over to cop."

"I believe you. Bro, trust me we about to get to a big bag." Top walked out the apartment, thinking about giving Gage five more keys, putting him at five left in the stash. He planned to break everything fifty-fifty with Body, but the only concern Top had right now was getting some more product some way.

***

North Hampton, L.I.

Mark's thirteen thousand square foot mansion looked like a crib outta some type of magazine. It was so nice, classy, and spacious. He had five bedrooms, three bathrooms, two walk-in closets, a living room upstairs and downstairs.

The backyard had a pool, bar, tennis court, gazebo, and entertainment area to host parties. Mark shared this beautiful home alone now. At one point he did have a wife, but unfortunately a few years back, her remains were found in Mexico near the border.

Till this day, Mark stressed over the thought of who'd killed his wife, but he had lots of enemies out there, so he couldn't place his lover's death on anybody.

Every day, Mark got an intense workout in before starting his day and today, he played tennis with the tennis ball launcher machine, spitting balls out at a fast pace while his maids prepared breakfast.

A lot later, he was supposed to have a sit down with one of his main clients, then Mark had to fly to Colombia. Mark dealt with drugs lords in Colombia and knew very powerful people out here. Even though he looked white, Mark was more Spanish than anything and spoke it well.

There were a couple of kingpins on the rise in New York and Mark didn't like it. He knew for a fact if Moss was still alive, he would easily take care of the problems. Mark missed Moss daily, he was a good person and stood on his word. Mark wished there were more dudes out there like him.

***

Fordham, The Bronx

Body double parked and ran in a store to grab some pain relievers for his head, he wasn't feeling good. Going in the store, he saw Steel coming out talking on his cell phone.

"Body, what's up, little cousin?" Steel saw him looking up and down, seeing Body fly in his Amiria outfit.

"Chilling or some shit." Body never had a close bond with his cousin from his uncles on Moss' side because he ever knew them. Body would just see them from time to time.

"How is Jalisa?" Steel asked.

Working, you know how she do." Body peeped Steel's Cuban link chain and bust down Rolex watch shining on his wrist.

"That's what's up, holla at me," Steel said before climbing in his Benz truck, the new G wagon.

Body wondered how Steel got to where he was at so fast, because four months ago when he saw Steel, boy looked fucked up.

Top called his cell phone asking him where he was at, and Body hung up because talking on the phone was a big no.

***

Soundview, The Bronx

Top saw Body get out his car in front of a middle school they both attended growing up. "We don't do cell phones, bro."

"Fuck all dat. I got most of the money, bro, but we need more product or to find a plug."

"Damn, already? that shit musta been good, but fuck finding a plug when we can just rob or kidnap one," Body suggested, and Top was down.

"You got someone in mind?"

73

"Yeah and no," Body responded to Top.

"What the fuck that means?"

"I'ma do my research then get back to you, bro." Body got in his car to pick up Mickey, thinking about the name Rock- O.

Chapter 17

Downtown Brooklyn

Rock-O drove through the bright city which sometimes seemed so dark, but he knew that was a part of the New York lifestyle of a street nigga. All he knew growing up in Bed-Stuy and Red Hook was money, murder and violence, gangs, prison, and to live for today not tomorrow.

Working with J-Baby for the past couple of years had been a blessing, he ran into her fight after his five-year state bid. She put him on a big bag, so he appreciated her in every way. She had his loyalty. "The money that was stolen, Rock-O replaced today. I took most of his stash, but he had to do the right thing and still conduct straight business."

Meeting with Jalisa at a funeral home was kinda odd, but he never questioned her meeting locations, because Rock-O respected the way he moved.

Rock-O remembered when Jalisa told him she moved weight, he laughed so hard he had tears. Later that same night, she handed him five kilos of coke.

Parking in the lot, Rock-O peeped J-Baby's Range flashing her headlights at him.

Rock-O took the bag of money with him, looking around to make sure the coast was clear. Lately, the feds been snatching niggas up all over the city and bring down big indictments.

"J Baby, what's up?"

"Rock-O, you know you don't gotta call me that. You family, dummy," Jalisa told him as Rock-O placed the big bag in her backseat.

"I know, but that name fits you."

Boy please, how's my sister?" Jalisa and her sister had a rocky relationship, but they spoke at times.

"My mom cool, working and still drinking crazy."

"Uhmmm, how's business?" She wanted to know because they never talked on phones, they only sent texts with locations and times to meet up.

"Shit looking real nasty out here right now, cuz I'ma be honest."

"What's goin on?"

"Someone robbed and killed my top worker. I had to sure the money in my stash to come see you today," he admitted, feeling ashamed as if he didn't know how to handle business int the streets.

"You have a clue who did it?"

"That's the whole thing. I coulda been anybody, got some ops and haters out there. It coulda been my own brother or soldiers," Rock-O stated, everybody a potential threat.

"Well, move smarter and on point. I respect how you made sure I got paid first, that said a lot about our character."

"Facts."

"Next time, I'll throw something extra in for you," she told him.

"That's love, but what's up with the re-up?" Rock-O had niggas waiting all over the city.

"It's in your shed behind your home."

"Again, I hope nobody saw the dropoff, my fucking neighbors are nosy."

"My people move like mice, no worries."

"Cool, my girl pregnant. I just found out, so I'm bout to step my shit up." Rock-O found out his girl Avany was knocked up four days ago.

"Congratulations, cuz. I'm happy for you but being a parent ain't as easy as people make it out to be, 'specially living a double life. trust me I know."

"Nah, you're right, it's gonna take time," he replied reaching for the door handle.

"Be safe, remember what I told you, cuz," Jalisa stated.

"I'm on it." Rock-O hopped out and got back into his car pulling off on his way to a section called Bushwick.

***

Bushwick, Brooklyn

Pulling up to the nice two-story home he rented out money was on his mind heavy odee. Rock-O needed to get the drugs outta his backyard shed and on the streets before the night ended, it was already 9:30 p. m.

Avany was hogtied on the floor, with duct tape around her mouth and two gunmen.

"Rock-O, right?" asked Body, now taking off his ski mask.

Rock-O thought the kid looked like his little cousin Nick, who he hadn't seen in over twelve years, since he was a baby.

"Y'all ain't have to violate like this, bra," Rock-O, said seeing Top take off his mask.

"I ain't know there was limits to this shit, son," said Top, pointing his gun at Rock-O who looked at his pregnant girlfriend crying non-stop.

"Listen dog, I have been watching you for a few days and today is your day, fam." Body kept it real with him.

"My girl is pregnant bro, I got drugs in the back shed, let us live y'all can take all that shit." Rock-O knew he could get back the drugs, but his life was out of the question.

"We got a motto," Top stated, looking at Body.

"Leave no witnesses," said Body.

BLOC....

BLOC....

BLOC....

The slugs hit Rock-O in his chest, making him spin, struggle to breathe. Top stood over Rock-O fired two shots in his head.

"What about her?" Top pointed at Rock-O's girl who had her eyes closed, scared.

"Nah, she pregnant, son. Let's get the work and slide before someone call the police," Body said, turning on the stereo on loud before going out back to collect the drugs he saw two men place back there earlier. Body had been staking Rock-O out for days and today was the big hit.

Romell Tukes

Chapter 18

Soundview, The Bronx

Jalisa had to get up early so she could make sure Mickey got to school on time, because his teachers accused him of being late twice this week. She asked Mickey about it, and he played dumb, so Jalisa took it upon herself to bring him to school now.

Things at work been going great, last week she hired a gang of black women and men, as well as did a lot of firing. The majority white employed company was now black and the weekly reports had already risen because now a lot of black owned companies were opening accounts with the bank.

Climbing out of her queen size bed, she heard the news reporter on TV mention a gruesome murder in Brooklyn, so she turned it up. Jalisa listened to the news every morning and fell asleep to the news.

"This is Kimberly reporting live from Bushwick, where gruesome murder took place, leaving a man dead and his pregnant girlfriend alive. The man's name was Rakeem, but the streets knew him as Rock-O and so did NYPD. He was a known drug dealer, kingpin status we believe, and the killing was believed to be drug related. Rakeem's girlfriend witnessed the whole scene but told the local authorities the killers had masks on. If anybody has any information on this case, please contact Crime Stoppers or your local police department," the older white woman stated before the news switched over to sports.

Jalisa didn't know how to feel at the moment, but she'd taken a big loss, Rock–O been her go-to guy for years. Whoever did this had to be connected to the first robbery, now she became worried if someone was on to her.

"Mom?" Mickey knocked on the door to see if she was up.

"I'll be out there in a few minutes to brush your teeth and get dressed," she replied.

"Mommy, I'm not a kid anymore. I already did that and made my bed," Mickey said, walking off to go fuck with Body, who most likely was asleep.

"What the hell yo," Jalisa mumbled, thinking of a plan B. She still had a lot of coke to move, but now she needed workers and that was a dangerous field to go look in. Even though Rock-O was family, she learned to trust him over the years.

Now she felt as if starting over was the only option or retiring from the game. Her Miami plug loved her too much he wouldn't allow Jalisa to quit on him.

***

183rd, The Bronx

Top and Body linked up at an apartment he found today through Top's mom co-workers. The spot was nice, low-key, and spacious enough for them both, but there were mice inside the apartment, which was normal.

"What do you think?" Top asked, looking out the window from the third floor.

"It's cool until we find something else," Body looked around.

"Facts, or at least until we find another spot, my G, because I'm sick of living at Mommy's house, bro." Top made sense.

"Nah, this shit cool, bro. Let's put down a payment to cover security and six months' rent."

"We can do that shit today, but what about the kilos?"

"What do you mean?" Body looked confused.

"The forty bricks we just got, nigga, you forgot already?"

"That's you, bro, fifty-fifty same as always. I don't sell drugs." Body was against drug selling but didn't mind collecting money or profiting from it.

"I already know, big bro, but that's my line of work. You ain't been getting no hits lately?" Top referred to hits as money for murders.

"Not recently, but soon. Summertime is coming up and somebody gonna hit my line. You know I take pride in my work."

"You should let me go on missions with you from time to time."

"The people normally request for me to go alone. The less the better, my guy," Body stated, walking outside noticing a BMW coupe that he had been seeing all day following him around.

"Yo son, is it me or is the white BMW with tints on our body right now?" Top must have read Body's mind.

"Follow my lead." Body walked toward the parked BMW as if he was walking down the block.

Looking through the front window, Body saw movement. Body could tell she wasn't police or a federal agent from her stare, but he wanted to know why she was tailing them.

Stopping at the driver's side window, Body knocked two times and she rolled down her window slowly.

"Why are you following us?" Body asked, looking into the woman's beautiful eyes.

"I'm only following you. I have no real concerns for your friend there, with all due respect, sir," the Spanish woman replied softly with a legit accident.

"How can I help you?" Body never saw the lady a day in his life, so he felt a little odd.

"May I speak to you in private for a second?" she requested.

"You straight? I'ma post up in the car." Top gave Body a reassuring look, letting him know he had his back.

"I'm Gucci, gang." Body walked to the passenger side, climbing in wondering what was on her mind.

"Thank you and I hope I don't spook you out by following y'all, but I had to make sure the person I was looking for is you." She dug in her purse.

Body had one hand close to his weapon, just in case the lady tried any slick shit.

"I'm the right person?"

"I know so. Body, a few months ago, you did work for this woman there, she is a friend of mine." The lady handed Body a picture.

"Don't know her, sorry." Body handed her back the pictures, not knowing if she was police or what now, because she knew a lot.

"The code was TB112," she said, now getting Body's attention.

Every client he dealt with had a private code. He would give it to them to remember if they referred him to someone or wanted more murders done.

"Ok talk, who are you and what do you want?" Body got straight to the point.

"My name is Cyn Gomez and I want you to kill my boyfriend," Cyn said, showing no type of emotion.

"What's his name?"

"Rosario, and I must say this will not be an easy task," she confirmed.

"Why do you think that?" Body wanted to laugh because he hadn't come across a hard kill yet.

"He's very powerful, Body."

"So am I. but give me your number and I will call you with a price in a few days," Body told her as she wrote down her number on a piece of paper. He got out of the car, not knowing what he'd just gotten himself into.

Chapter 19

Millbrook PJ's, The Bronx

Ice took the elevator downstairs to meet Steel, who was in the neighborhood already. Ice had a young bitch on the fourth floor he was fucking with for a month now. shawty was a dancer and about her bag, so Ice took homegirl under the wing.

When the elevator doors opened, he saw Steel standing in the lobby rapping to an older chick with a wagon.

"Steel, do that shit on your own time," Ice said, scaring the woman away.

"Damn bro, she was about to tell me to come upstairs"

"Nigga, I just saved you from a STD. Thank me later, thirsty nigga." Ice walked outside.

"Won't be the first time or last," Steel confirmed as Ice gave him a nasty look.

"What's so important you had to pull me outta some pussy, son? I'm out here in fucking slippers." Ice looked down at his flip flops.

"Who you know in the building?"

"Nigga, what the fuck do you want?" Ice got frustrated.

"The work," Steel said, lightly shaking his head.

"What about it? Speak nigga, I can't read your mind"

"It's trash, bro, the shit not even coming back when niggas cook it."

"You sure the right people cooking it and know what they doing?" Ice was making sure because he never had any issues before today with the product.

"I cooked that shit myself, fam, and lost mostly all of it. The coke had to be cut at least three to four times."

"Damn, it's that bad?" Ice believed him now and he knew his boy woulda been down with the pack by now.

"Bro, fiends ain't even coping from our people everybody going to Burnside." Steel been hearing about a nigga named Gage pushing some fire within Burnside.

"How much do you got left?"

"Fourteen birds"

"Give all of that to Lil Elvis, because I'll drop them shits back off with the rest, bro." Ice couldn't believe his plug gave him some dirt work that was stepped on.

"Copy, say less." Steel walked off, upset he wasted his time trying to sell trash work.

***

Highbridge, The Bronx

Top drove outta Highbridge smiling because he linked up with his boy King H, who just came home from the Island after fighting a robbery and attempt murder charge, which he beat. Body also knew King H. They all went to middle school together.

"This shit nice, bro," King H said in the passenger seat of the Audi coupe enjoying the nice day outside.

"I copped this joint a few weeks ago, son."

"You said when we was on Rikers Island you was gonna come home and hop in some fly shit." King H remembered Top in the dayroom, talking bout how he was gonna hop in something foreign when he touched.

In jails, niggas talked shit all day about what they had or what they planned to get, but most niggas lied.

"Yeah, homie. We stars so niggas gotta move like bosses."

"Facts son, but yo I'ma keep it a band, blood. The jail is talking," King H stated.

"About what?" Top made a left down a one-way.

"Niggas saying your boy Body out here putting everything to sleep or the low." King H used to hear crazy stories about Body all day some he couldn't believe because Body was always the cool quiet kid. King H was always loud, in trouble, and wilding out for no reason.

"You know, bro."

"I heard about Natural. This has fucked me up, she was my ex." King H used to be in love with Natural in school.

84

"That was family. When I find out who did it, bro. I'ma push the button on the bitch ass nigga," said King H, thinking about the night he cried in the cell after hearing about Natural's death.

"Montay did that shit, my nigga. I'ma take boy head off when I see him, word to my dead bro," Top replied, on his way to a shopping area so he could pick up King H some gear, because coming home to nothing was hard itself and getting back on your feet.

"I had a feeling that hoe ass nigga had something to do with it. The whole jail knows about y'all beef, and that nigga killed my big cousin last year, son. I'm forever on that nigga ass, no homo," said King H, because it sounded a little freaky.

"I'ma catch son."

"We bros, you know me, Top. Fam, I'm rockin with you and Body, y'all like family." King H really had genuine love for the gang.

"Say that, boy, and we out here doing bad things," Top said, driving in the crazy Bronx traffic bumper to bumper.

"Oh yeah, y'all getting to it?"

"Big facts. I wanted to speak with you after we went shopping, but now seems like the perfect time."

"Ok, about what?"

"Moving these keys in Highbridge, so you basically run that shit out here." Top told the truth because King H was the most feared and respected youngest nigga out there with a team of hitters.

"Bricks?" King H wanted to make sure he heard clearly.

"Yeah nigga, shit change since you been in word to me."

"I'm down, bro. I gotta get on my feet, son. The bro A Boogie Wit the Hoodie tossed me a Rolex and chain, but I gotta go to a bag." King H knew how to get chicken, he just never had a plug.

"We lit tonight, it's on," Top assured him, happy to have a new member on the team.

Romell Tukes

Chapter 20

Bay Plaza Mall, The Bronx

Body called Cyn to see if she could meet him in the mall parking lot so they could go over the details. Body had no clue who the person was, why Cyn wanted him dead, nor did he care at all. He just needed his money.

The BMW parked next to him and she got out. This was the first time he saw her full body and Cyn's ass was crazy. Body couldn't believe how stacked up Cyn really was, he wondered how much she paid to get her body done.

"Hey, Body." Cyn climbed in the car, smelling good with her long hair in a ponytail.

"How's it going?"

"Fine, are you ready?" she asked.

"That's why I'm here."

"The guy's name is Mojoa, he lives in Miami at a lovely mansion in Miami-Dade County."

"Miami?" Body repeated, he never did jobs outside of New York.

"Yes, he is a big supplier out there, but I need him dead and I will give you a quarter-million dollars," Cyn said, pulling a hundred twenty-five grand out her Birkin bag.

"Hold on, you sure you have that much money?" Body said, looking at the wad of blue faces in her hand.

"Yes, this is half, the rest will be given on your arrival back. No games on my behalf, I've heard good things about you, that's why I chose you."

Body had never done a hit over a hundred grand, so this much money overwhelmed him at the moment.

"You got all the info?"

"Yes, and I will have an Uber pick you up from the airport with two guns at hand for you," she confirmed.

"No problem, you really had this planned out, I see."

"Yes, every dog has their day. Call me when you get back, handsome." Cyn handed Body the piece of paper and kissed him on the cheek.

When she left, Body thought about the whole situation, and he started to think about who Cyn really was. Body felt like someone sent her to him, but the way she moved, he knew Cyn could have been trying to make some power moves.

He made a mental note to look into Cyn when he came back from his trip. Body went home to book a flight and he didn't plan to take clothing with him.

He thought about telling Top, but Body figured it would be best not to, at least until he come back.

***

Soundview, The Bronx

Walking into his mom's house, he saw her on the phone. Body still didn't get a chance to tell his mother he moved out, *but right now would be a good time*, he thought.

"What's up, Mom?" Body said when she hung up the phone.

"Hey baby, where you been?" Jalisa asked, fresh outta work.

"I moved out," Body managed to get to his mouth.

"Ok, you're back but pack a bag, we are going on a trip to Miami for my birthday tomorrow." Jalisa caught him by surprise, but he totally forgot her birthday was tomorrow.

"Oh ok, I can't wait." Body couldn't believe the timing.

"Pack up, we leave at 7:00 am," she said before going to her room.

Body sat on the living couch and tried to put some shit together in his head, such as when he could bust his move and still enjoy Miami and Jalisa's birthday.

***

The next morning, Body was up and ready. He spent the night at his mom's crib so they would leave early.

"You coming too?" Mickey asked, faking like he was mad.

"Yeah why, little nigga?"

"Just asking. I love Spring Break because we got no school." Mickey jumped up and down.

"Everybody ready?" Jalisa came downstairs in a sundress and Chanel sunglasses, looking pretty.

"Yes," Mickey said as the Uber blew the horn outside.

They got to JFK Airport in forty minutes, a reasonable time due to the heavily backed-up traffic. Jalisa already had the tickets and their plane had five minutes to take off, so they barely made it on time.

The whole plane ride, Body stared out his window, thinking about how he was gonna shake his family for at least an hour. Jalisa and Mickey dozed off for a few hours until their flight landed at Miami International Airport.

"I was knocked out." Jalisa laughed as they walked through the crowd to get their bags.

"Me too," Mickey said, ripping the curse out his eyes.

"Our bags right there." Body started snatching the bags off the baggage claim carousel.

"Thanks baby, we gonna have so much fun," Jalisa boasted with joy because she hadn't seen a vacation in years.

"Here go a cab." Body saw a cab pull up and rushed it, throwing the bags inside the trunk when the driver opened it. Seeing Jalisa and Mickey get inside, he made his move closing the door.

"You getting in?" Jalisa asked.

"Yeah... I'ma meet y'all at the hotel, Mom. I ain't bring no clothes. I'ma pick up an outfit and shoes." Body didn't bring a bag on purpose for this reason.

"We will all get together," Mickey added.

"I'll be back shortly, love y'all," Body told them, looking at the cab driver so he could pull off.

"Ok, be safe," Jalisa said, she already knew he had money on him because it stuck out his pockets.

When the cab pulled off, Body called the number on the paper Cyn gave him and waited for the Uber, hoping his plan goes well.

It didn't take long for the Uber, a black Benz truck pulled up with tints. Body assumed that was it, because the guy said a black truck.

Body got inside to see a middle-aged Dominican man with a scar on his face.

"Body, right?" the driver asked.

"Yes."

The Uber driver handed Body a small bag with a set of house keys and two 9mm, fully loaded handguns. Body thought the job seemed too good to be true, but he followed the program.

Without giving the driver the address, he knew where to go, which made Body a little uncomfortable.

Dade County had beautiful mansions with nice grass and long driveways.

"Park a block up." Body didn't want to get out onto same block as the victim's house.

"Ok, I'll be waiting here." The driver did as Body asked, parking a block away from Mojoa's crib.

Body got out, in his zone and marched right up the block, until he saw the amazing mansion that looked like it had two sides and two complexes.

Body walked up the driveway, looking at a row of luxury cars, Rolls Royce, Benz, Bentley's, Lambo's and a Bugatti. There was no camera in sight, which didn't make sense, so Body got a little nervous.

At the front door, he placed the key in and slowly opened it, to hear Spanish music playing loudly from the living room area. Body pulled out his guns taking the safety off, not knowing what was waiting around the corner.

Body saw Mojoa sniffing coke off a glass table, while two sexy skinny women danced on top of it to the music. The party was so litty Body wanted to join but instead, he fucked it up.

BOC....

BOC....

BOC....
BOC....
BOC....
BOC....
BOC....
BOC....

Body emptied four rounds in Mojoa's head and then mercilessly murdered all of the others, before walking out, dancing to the Spanish music blasting.

Romell Tukes

Chapter 21

Miami, FL

Next Day

Jalisa woke up early after a fun night with Body. She wished Brooklyn could have come, but unfortunately schoolwork had her tied up. But Jalisa was so proud of her only daughter trying to make something of herself, unlike most women these days chasing clout.

The hotel they stayed at was called the Blu Fountainbleau, and Jalisa loved it. There was so much fun shit to do inside, from partying, entertainment and restaurants to the swimming area next to the gyms.

She peeped her head in Mickey's room to see him snoring, which was good because he would normally wake up around 1:00 to 2:00 pm anyway on weekends. Body's room was connected to his, so she walked inside to smoke weed, but Jalisa knew her son would experience it as soon as she did at his age.

Jalisa saw a red dot on the lower part of Body's Air Forces. She assumed it was nothing of concern, so she paid it no mind and went about her business.

Outside, she called an Uber to take her to an important meeting. Her main reason for coming to Miami was to have fun family time and meet with her plug, who already had her one-point-seven million dollars for the next shipment order.

Ten minutes later a cab arrived, and Jalisa got inside, rocking a Fendi sweatsuit with matching running shoes. Her connect did not live far, so the ride was about twelve minutes to the fabulous home she admired. Next year, she planned to move out The Bronx to Long Island or somewhere like New Jersey, in an upscale neighborhood with expensive homes only the rich could afford.

Jalisa got out and walked up to the rotary, ringing the bell while hearing music playing. She never had to call the connect because they had a good relationship. After five minutes, she took it upon herself to walk inside and there was a funny smell coming from the living room area.

Jalisa walked right into a death trap. Her plug, Mojoa's head had bullet holes, and two naked bitches laid on the floor behind the table dead with blood everywhere.

The first thing that came to her mind was her payment. She'd sent it to him, but Mojoa always placed the money in oversea accounts, so Jalisa knew it was a loss.

She was so furious, Jalisa kicked Mojoa in his nuts before leaving. *Too much shit been taking place*, Jalisa thought, *is someone onto me, because this been hitting close to home.*

***

Castle Hill, The Bronx

King H just copped a new Acura coupe to get around in and make his moves. Top blessed him with a couple of bricks the other day and they were almost gone. Highbridge was a gold mine and King H planned to look it down.

"King, I'm hungry," a slim, cute brown-skinned chick said in the passenger seat.

"I'm bout to take you home anyway."

"Please baby, you been fucking me all night. I'm starving," she whined.

"For some dick," he joked.

"Ha ha ha, not funny, babe."

"I got cha." King H saw a Wing Stop Chicken spot to his right and she loved their pepper lemon wings.

Pulling over, he parked behind a BMW sedan with rims and tints. King H couldn't wait to get his foreign car, he just wanted to save some paper first.

"What do you want?"

"Buffalo wings, a twenty-piece and mild wings for my kids. I know they hungry," she stated about to keep requesting orders for her mom and brother, but he hopped out of the car.

About to reach for the door, King H couldn't believe who he ran into coming out.

"Welcome home, big bro," Montay said smiling, about to embrace King H, but the look on his face made Montay uncomfortable.

"You bitch ass nigga," King H yelled, reaching for his gun from his waistband.

Montay pushed King H into the door and dropped his good bag reaching for his gun, close to the BMW.

BOC....

BOC....

BOC....

BOOM....

BOOM....

Both of them fired at each other ducking and missing, the blazing fire hitting their cars as the civilians inside the food spot took cover.

Montay fired twice more and got in his BMW racing off, King H did the same but when he entered his car, his female friend was dead, bleeding out the neck. He pushed the lady outside, leaving her on the curb, speeding off and thinking of a way to get rid of the Acura, because somebody would give the police details of his car.

King H called Top while he entered the Soundview section, which was a few blocks down from Castle Hill. Most hoods close to each other in The Bronx stuck together as a unit to war with other hoods, but not Soundview and Castle Hill, shit was litty.

"Yurrooooo," Top answered.

"I just saw old boy and shit got a little nasty, boy."

"Who dat?"

"Montay."

"Oh shit, you got son?" asked Top.

"Nah bro, I'm sick."

"No worries. I got a plan, where you at though?"

"In your hood"

"Pull up to Story Avenue. I'm at the corner store, bro. the dice game popping right now, son," Top stated.

"Say that. I'm down the block." King H figured he'd ditch the car when he got to Top's block, and wipe the shit down to be safe.

Chapter 22

Washington Heights, NY

Body called Cyn as soon as he touched down in the city to figure things out about the rest of his pay. Something about the kill didn't seem right at all with him, but he tried to overlook it.

He wouldn't normally ask questions but today he had a few for Cyn. Leaving Miami, his mom had a fucked-up attitude, he didn't understand how she could quickly go from happy to mad, but Body knew women had their periods, and blamed it on that.

A BMW pulled up behind him and Cyn hopped out in work-out gear with a brown paper bag in hand.

"Hey, you." Cyn spoke, getting inside filling the car with her perfume.

"What's the energy?"

"Everything is great, bout to go hit the gym. How was your trip?" She already knew the answer because Cyn got word on Mojoa's death days ago.

"I did it the first day I arrived in Miami, and it was a little too easy."

"I told you the shit would be like taking candy from a baby," she replied smiling.

"Guess so."

"Here goes the rest, a hundred twenty-five grand, thank you for your work." She passed him the money and he only looked through the healthy stack.

"Thanks."

"Is everything ok?" She got a weird vibe off him.

"Who was he?"

"Mojoa?"

"No, Harry Potter," Body responded back in a funny manner.

"He was a kingpin who helped kill my brother, any more questions?" Cyn now had a little attitude she hated to explain herself.

He replied, "12A4401."

"What?" She looked confused.

"That's your code in case you refer me or need me again."

"Ok, got it. I may be calling you sooner than later," Cyn stated, getting out.

Body couldn't help but to take a peek at her phat ass jiggling in leggings. She was a different type of bitch, and he was feeling her.

Tomorrow, he had a date with Hope. They'd been FaceTiming and texting a lot, but that wasn't enough. Body needed some pussy. He just realized his dick had been in the sand for a few weeks.

***

Queens, NY

Steel had a little young chick in the Jamaica Queens section who was trying to get a little money, so Steel came out to check.

Driving down a middle-class block, Steel saw Kayna's car in her mom's driveway and beeped the horn. It was a hot spring day and Steel wanted to get his car washed, then go check on his trap in The Bronx.

The thought of seeing Body a few weeks ago rubbed him wrong, even though that was his cousin, Steel didn't see it as such.

"Open the door." Kayna popped up outta nowhere, wearing denim shorts showing her lack of curves, but a phat pussy print.

"My bad, ma. I see you out here in your open toe sandals." Steel looked at her manicured feet.

"You know how a bitch does, but what's up with you?"

"Came to see how I can help."

"In a lot of ways," she shot back, really needing some money because she was late on bills and school tuition. And she needed new clothes for summer.

"Starting from?"

"I know some coke heads are around the corner I came up with, they be spending some paper too," she confirmed.

"You need work?"

"Yes, just until I get on my feet, then I'll start copping."

"Ok bet. I'ma toss you two hundred grams that's all you and four bandz to get on your feet, ma. I fucks with you," he lied.

"Damn, I see," she said, licking her phat lips.

"Tomorrow's good."

"Yep," she said, rubbing his inner thigh, reaching for his zipper as he leaned back surprised.

She pulled his dick out, kissed it up and down before taking it deep in her mouth.

"God damn" Heh moaned as she started to bop quickly using her lips.

Kaysha sucked his manhood until he shot a load down her throat as she swallowed every drop.

"I'll see you tomorrow," she smiled and got out walking back inside.

Steel rethought about giving her the work and money that fast, because he never came so quickly, he felt a little embarrassed.

***

Soundview, The Bronx

"Where have you been at, bro?" asked Top, rolling a blunt of loud in his new car, because the window shattered on the other ride, after the shootout with a masked man last night leaving a party.

"Miami to handle business."

"Damn, and you ain't invite me, bro? I know you saw a bunch of bitches," Top stated.

"Facts, but like I said it was business. How is everything moving with you?" Body saw a text from Hope appear on his phone.

"Shit moving. I got King H down with us now, this nigga got into a crazy shootout in Castle Hill recently."

"Damn, bro a real one, we need more niggas like him to make this shit work," Body added.

"Speaking of work, soon we gonna need more."

"Ok, I am trying to see what I can come up with."

"Me too, bro. Facts," Top said, smoking the blunt, in his thoughts.

Romell Tukes

Chapter 23

Harlem, NY

Jalisa drove out to Harlem because Ms. Dee said she wasn't feeling well at all today, so Jalisa took off from work to take her mother to the hospital if needed.

Since losing Rock-O and her connection, things have been hard to figure out, but she did have some emergency work stashed for a rainy day but today wasn't that day.

Getting out to find a new plug was scary like Halloween, because niggas moving big weight were setting their clients up left and right in New York.

Jalisa knew a dude in Atlanta she went to school with, doing big things. Word was, he supplied the majority of Atlanta. The only thing was, the nigga really had a crush on Jalisa and fat niggas weren't her type at all. She had a thing for dark-skinned niggas with their weight up.

Parking in front of her mom's house, she just remembered tomorrow is Brooklyn's birthday, so she wanted to surprise with a gift. Jalisa wanted to get her daughter a red Birkin bag.

Making plans to hit the Birkin bag store in White Plains Mall upon leaving her mom's house, she couldn't wait. Plus, she wanted to get Mickey some new sneakers for the summertime, he was growing out of them.

Once upstairs, she used her spare key to get inside.

"Mommy?"

"Jalisa, I'm in the living room, honey," Ms. Dee yelled watching a rerun of *Good Times.*

"How are you feeling?" Jalisa walked in on her mom laying on the couch, wrapped up in a blanket.

"No baby, my fever is getting worse."

"You need to go to the hospital?" Jalisa could tell her mom didn't feel well from the look on her face.

"Yeah baby, Mommy feeling dizzy," she stated, slowly getting up so she could head to the hospital with her daughter.

"Come on, let me help you." Jalisa helped her mom up from the couch, then the weirdest thing happened.

BOOM

The front door got kicked in as men in FBI coats rushed the crib. "Freeze, FBI," the agents yelled.

Ms. Dee took off like a track star, running to the back room as agents followed her.

Jalisa was body slammed to the floor like a pro wrestler.

"Got you now, you little bitch, your queen pin days are over," a big white agent said, placing a knee on Jalisa's neck.

"Suck my dick," Jalisa shouted as gunfire erupted from the back room.

"Man down, man down, she went out the window down the fire escape," two agents yelled, coming back out.

"Call medical and back up right now," another agent yelled, rushing downstairs to catch Ms. Dee, who was wanted for two murders that took place twenty years ago.

Thirty minutes later, Ms. Dee was detained, and Jalisa was too, but her mom had killed a federal agent and injured another one, so now Ms. Dee had two more federal charges.

***

Soundview, The Bronx

Body got a call from Mickey at home, asking him to come by because their mom didn't come home from work. He came from Tremont fucking with Hope, who was at her family crib. The two had been spending a lot of time together.

"Mickey." Body entered his mom's house which had new carpet.

"Coming," he replied with a kid's voice.

"Where is Mom anyway?" asked Body when Mickey got downstairs.

"I don't know, she not picking up" he called his mom on his cell phone, but Jalisa's phone went to voicemail.

Body was about to call until he got a call from a blocked number, so he answered.

"You have a federal call from Jalisa," the phone receiver stated. As Body heard his mom's voice, he walked outside so Mickey couldn't hear what was going on.

"Mom, why are you in jail?"

"Baby, take Mickey to my cousin Candy's house in Brooklyn until you turn eighteen, make sure he is good," Jalisa said.

"What happened?" He heard panic in his mom's voice which was way subnormal.

"I don't want to talk about it over the phone, ok? But I love you, ok? Get a fake ID saying you're eighteen years old, son. You can come see me, we need to talk," she said with a lot of noise in the background.

"Ok. Mom, where is Grandma? I can bring Mickey over there," Body stated.

"No! Grandma in the hospital and she'll be here when she get out," Jalisa said sadly.

"I'm confused, Mom."

"No need to... believe me. I'm in MDC Brooklyn, ok? Call Brooklyn and tell her I love her. I'm sorry," Jalisa said as the phone hung up. Body looked inside the house and saw Mickey's puppy dog eyes. Explaining to him what was going on would be hard because he didn't even know what was happening.

"That was Mommy?" Mickey asked.

"Yes, and you gotta pack up some clothes and toys, we going to Brooklyn."

"Can I bring my game?" Mickey smiled.

"Yes, we going to Candy's house."

"Travis and Shell mom? I hate them. They always break my games," cried Mickey sitting on the stairs protesting.

"Listen, it's just for a few days, ok?"

"Days? Where is Mommy?" Mickey asked.

"Vacation, kid, now get ready." Body went to look out the windows to make sure the feds was not outside because he knew Jalisa called from the feds.

"We just came from a vacation." Mickey wasn't letting up at all.

"Mickey, stop questioning me and pack your shit." Body was starting to get upset because his little brother wasn't listening.

Mickey ran upstairs crying, knowing there was something wrong with his momma. Body could not believe his mom and grandma was in the feds, he figured it was from taxes or some type of mistake.

Body planned to get a fake ID tomorrow from Top's cousin, who knew how to do all that fraud shit.

Chapter 24

Manhattan, NY

Mark climbed out the back of a Maybach as his personal driver opened the door for him.

"Thank you. Give me thirty minutes or less, then I have to attend another meeting in New Jersey," Mark told his driver.

"Yes sir," the driver replied, standing at attention as if he was still in the Army.

Mark only kept enforcement around him that was specially trained in combat and war, trained to kill just in case something was to go down at any given moment.

The brisk air hit Mark hard as he made his way into the upscale restaurant, while buttoning up his Armani blazer.

Coming out for a business lunch hadn't been in Mark's plans, but his top clientele explained over the phone it was an emergency due to a serious situation. Walking inside, a waiter led him to his guest, rich white people gave Mark smiles and head nods, thinking he was one of them. But he was far from white or legit.

"This better be fucking good," Mark said in a low tone to Papa, who had to be the only Latino man present in a suit.

"Someone killed my brother." Papa's face had a saddened look, as if Mark played a role in his brother's death.

"What? When? I just sent him the order down there. I took a fucking loss, you're telling me?" Mark's voice raised.

"The money and drugs we can get back, but my brother we can't, Mark."

"I don't give a shit about your brother, this is a business, not *The Brady Bunch*. We need to find out who did this and if there is any connection to us."

"Mark, it seems to me you only care about yourself. We brought you a lot of money for decades and you show no respect." Papa wasn't feeling Mark's resonance.

"Let me tell you something. I only care about my business. True, you and your brother brought me a ton of money but I'm the reason you and Mojoa got rich. If it wasn't for me, the both of you woulda been in Mexico, cleaning horse shit for a living, so you need to show me respect before you end up like Mojoa but in a worse condition." Mark got serious and Papa smiled at the disrespect, but Mark meant every word.

"I didn't come down near to argue with my friend. I just want to figure this out. My people in Miami are on it as we speak. I just figured to tell you in person, boss." Papa took a deep breath, controlling his anger and putting his emotion to the side.

"You know Mojoa's clients?"

"No, but I can find out. I know he had a black book with everybody he dealt with in there."

"Start there and find out if he had any enemies," Mark suggested, before getting up to leave.

"Tonight, everything will be in place?" Papa asked about his load coming in.

"I'm going to Jersey right now." Mark left Papa sitting there.

Papa started to think whether Mark had something to do with Mojoa's death because his reaction was off. Mojoa was Papa's blood brother, and they came to New York for a new way of life, and they found it when they met Mark one day while working on his lawn cutting grass. Mark showed them a new life of tricks and money. When Mojoa moved to Miami to take over Papa was against it, but Mojoa wanted his own empire, so he relocated and built one. But now he was gone, and Papa wanted blood.

***

MDC Federal Jail, Brooklyn

Days Later

Jalisa couldn't believe what her life had turned into within a matter of days. The feds charged her with narcotics, racketeering, 924(0), conspiracy to commit murder, and a bunch of other serious charges that could put her away for life.

A police officer escorted her to the visitation room for her first visit. She wore brown jumpers like the rest of the inmates. Since her prison stay, she hadn't said a word to anybody in fear of who they might be. The guards told Jalisa not to speak about her case, because of the high population of rats.

Her mom was in the next unit, fool tripping over the murder charges she was facing. Jalisa told her mom through the door last night to be strong, they'd be fine once she got them lawyers.

The visitation room was quiet and only four people out here visited with family members. Body was ducked off in the back when she saw him. Jalisa smiled, looking at her handsome baby. She rushed to hug her boy, trying to hold down the tears building up inside.

"Mom, what happened?" was all Body could fix his mouth to say.

"I did wrong, honey. I'ma be honest. When your dad got killed, he left me a lot of drugs to sell so I could take care of y'all. I did just that for us to have a good life, now it caught up with me. I'm facing some serious time. Your grandma is for some shit she did years ago" Jalisa gave it to him raw and upfront.

"This shit is crazy what should I do?"

"Get lawyer and I want you to go alone to 979 Church Avenue, apartment 5B in Brooklyn the key is on top of the door frame, check the kitchen and everything will make sense," she told him.

"I haven't been to sleep since your arrest. Brooklyn wanna drop outta school, and Mickey cries every day, he keep getting sent back home from school."

"I know, baby, this shit hurts but you have to be the backbone of the family. It's time you step up and become a man," her words hit Body like an eighteen-wheeler.

"I will, Mom, I swear."

"Be smart out there and watch your back, carry on the family name. I know the thing you was doing, I sent someone to you for a job you did in Mount Vernon. You're just like your father." She smiled, seeing how shocked he was.

Romell Tukes

Chapter 25

Manhattan, NY

Upon leaving the jail visit, Body was filled with all types of emotions, from rage to disappointment. Never in a million years would he believe his mom sold drugs if she didn't relate to him openly.

Seeing Jalisa in a prison uniform made Body really want to tighten up and get on his shit, so he promised himself today he would be on a different type of time.

The first thing on his to-do list was get a lawyer so he Googled the best federal lawyer in New York City and came up with a man named Mr. Goldenberg from Manhattan. He needed to get his mom and grandma outta prison whatever cost. Hearing his grandma's charges broke his heart and now he knew why she was always paranoid daily, it made sense.

Parking in a garage area across from Goldenberg Law Firm, he tried to add up all the money he already had saved up. But he couldn't remember because he was spending money left and right.

Walking into the lawyer's office the place was empty besides the assistant, who sat up from reading a magazine.

"Good afternoon, how can I help you?" the pretty older white woman asked with a very warm smile.

"Is Mr. Goldenberg in?"

"As a matter of fact, he is," she said, picking up the office phone, letting her boss know he got a visitor. "He said give him a few seconds, but you can have a seat if you like," the lady said hanging up, placing her head back into the mag.

Body saw a text from Brooklyn appear, asking did he go see Mommy and Body confirmed, letting her know he'd be calling within an hour.

"Step in my office," Mr. Goldenberg said, stepping foot out of his office in a clean suit. Mr. Goldenberg was a tall, slim, white guy with a bald head who loved golf and boat trips.

"I'm Nick and I need your help. My mom and grandma just got arrested for some serious charges, and I need your service." Body gave it to him raw.

"What's their names?" Mr. Goldenberg asked, while typing on his computer, wondering why the story sounded so familiar.

"Jalisa and…"

"Hold on, your grandma's name is Ms. Dee government Debra Cox?" the lawyer asked, looking at his computer screen.

"Yes."

"They're already on my caseload, young man. I'm going to visit them sometime this week to set up motions for their bail hearings," Mr. Goldenberg stated, clearing his throat.

"That's impossible."

"What?"

"I just came from a visit and my mom told me to find her a lawyer." Body looked confused.

"Well, they're both on my caseload. I'm going to MDC Brooklyn Federal holdover this week. Somebody must love them." The lawyer smiled.

"Who paid the fines?"

"It was a drop off, no-name client, but whoever it was paid the fine and some extra, so I will do my best to get your family outta jail or a low prison sentence, because they both have clean records." The lawyer had been working on all types of cases for twenty-seven years and had a good track record in the federal court system. Mr. Goldenberg was one of the most respectful federal lawyers in New York, and the most expensive.

"How much do you charge?"

"It depends on the case"

"How much did the person pay you to take the case?" Body wanted to know.

"I don't usually discuss prices with non-clients but since that's your mom, I'll bend my rules. It was four hundred grand dropped off, more than enough for my services." Mr. Goldenberg smiled, thinking about the new car he planned to buy with his profit.

"Wow." Body knew he wouldn't have been able to afford that price anyway, so whoever did it saved him a lot of time.

"Yep, so tell your family they're in good hands and have no worries. Even though the charges they are being accused of are serious, stemming from murders, racketeering, drugs, queen pin 848 status and a bunch of others, it's still workable," the lawyer assured him, making Body feel better.

"That's good news. I'll be in touch, shorty. Thank you for your time." Body stood to leave.

"Thank you, young man." Mr. Goldenberg went back to work on his computer.

Body left with all types of thoughts on his mind, like who would pay four hundred thousand for his mom and grandma's release, it didn't make sense to him.

***

Pace University, NY

Brooklyn found it hard to focus on college and her personal life at the moment, due to her current situation. She'd been locked in her room for two days, missing classes and not eating as much. The thought of her mom and grandma being in jail crushed everything inside of her.

At first, nobody would tell Brooklyn why her family was in jail, so she took it upon herself to Google their names and she could not believe what came up.

Seeing her mom being classified as a queen pin drug dealer and her grandma being labeled as a killer made Brooklyn sick. Growing up, she had the perfect life and when Moss died, Jalisa did her best to provide and raise Brooklyn correct, so what she was seeing online upset her for ruining the family name.

Waiting on Body to call back seemed like forever. She wanted to know what was going on. Brooklyn knew people who had loved ones to go to jail, but she never wondered how it affects the people on the outside, because nobody really cares about that. Brooklyn now truly understood how it felt to have someone close to you get locked up, it hurt deeply.

Chapter 26

Queens, NY

Ice came out to party with his crew to celebrate one of his young boy's birthday, who'd been doing the right thing for the gang in Queens, where Ice was getting money at since he was a young nigga.

Being in the strip club, throwing ones and tens made Ice feel like the boss he was, but he couldn't help but to think back to when being broke we all he knew. Coming from The Bronx with a brother like Moss, Ice had to put on and make his own path, or he would forever be in the shadows of his big brother.

The street law wasn't his first choice, Ice loved basketball and wanted to because an NBA star like his role model Allen Iverson, but the streets grabbed him up. Building a crew was the hardest shit to do and finding a drug connect everything else was about enforcement taking over blocks.

Meeting Papa was the best thing that ever happened to Ice, because his life changed for the better, taking over parts of the city building his dream team.

Seeing his crew ball, throwing money on the stage, popping bottles made Ice appreciate the finer things in life.

"I'm tryna leave with a few of these hoes tonight," Steel said, drinking Casa Migos lit leaning into Ice, who was sober all night.

"Don't you got a girl at home, dumb nigga?" Ice asked.

"Yeah, but tonight, I'm turning up."

"Ight, that bitch kick you out again and burn your clothes, don't call me" Ice said over the loud music. Steel started to think, because if he didn't come home, then his girlfriend would start acting crazy.

"Maybe you right, big bro." Steel looked at a young crowd of niggas who'd been throwing money nonstop, wilding in the spot.

"Who them little niggas?" asked Ice, peeping their swag all night.

"I don't know, but Blu said one of them is from Highbridge and boy gave it up," Steel confirmed, watching the movie because the whole club was litty as dancers got crazy all over the walls and stage, on the floor shit was going bananas.

"Highbridge, huh?" Ice looked through the crowd, wondering when the little niggas jumped off the porch.

"I'ma look into it."

"Say dat, but let's enjoy this night,'' Ice said, going back to partying.

***

King, Gage and Top all came out deep as hell, basically taking over half the club, violating the dancers by sticking fingers up their butts and pouring liquor on them.

Top invited them out to party in Queens because his boys been doing good, moving keys left and right. Body couldn't believe how fast King H and Gage was getting the bricks gone.

"Since you found a plug bro, my life been a fucking fairy tale" Gage stated, sipping Henny out the bottle.

"A plug who said I had a connect?" Top looked at Gage awkwardly.

"I don't know how you flooding the streets, bro. So, you gotta be connected to El Chapo, nigga," Gage joked.

"Nigga just out here trying to make it," Top explained, seeing King H on the couch with two dancers getting crazy at the same time, kissing each other trying to seduce him.

"You peep them old niggas over there watching our bop?" Gage pointed at Steel and Ice.

"Fuck them niggas. I been peeping them all night, but they not gonna do shit, we strapped up and got cutters, son. I wish a nigga would, on gang." Top got serious thinking about violence.

"Facts though, boy," Gage added, going back to drinking his Henny.

Top just so happened to see one of King H's boys arguing with two kids on the other side of the club with a stripper bitch in the middle, trying to calm shit down.

When Top hopped up and rushed through the crowd, so did Gage and his crew. Then, King H plus his goons were now on Top's heels.

By the time Top made it to the scene, all he heard was, "Suck my dick," then someone swung on King H's young boy, almost knocking him out but he caught his balance and started to get busy.

The club went up and Ice and Steel were doing the most, hitting niggas in the head with bottles, getting crazy. Steel saw Top doing two of his niggas dirty dolo and came behind him to choke him.

Top swiftly got out the chokehold, pulled out his gun and slapped Steel with it, before he turned to run.

Steel felt a burn hit his ass cheeks twice as shots went off in the club, making everybody go into chaos.

Ice saw Top shooting, then King H fired two shots, hitting Ice's close friend Sticks.

BOOM....

BOOM....

Not trying get killed in a club brawl, Ice and a few of his goons that weren't still fighting hit the back exit, as women screamed and cried out loud.

Top dashed out front with Gage and King H, pushing strippers out the way. Bitches were running in heels and some barefooted, trying to save their own lives.

Outsides cars were speeding and racing out the parking like a terrorist attack took place instead of a club shooting.

"Yo that shit was crazy, blood," King H yelled in the driver's seat of his new Range Rover.

"Top, you shot dude in the ass, son was stuck on the floor," Gage laughed.

"Them niggas clipped bad, bro. I hope he make it, Crane and Rock stayed with him, so he should be good," Top said, seeing a line of cop cars and ambulance trucks rush to the scene behind them.

"One of the nigga's name was Ice," Gage said.

"Whoever it was, shit lit now. I don't care where they from we on their ass" Top said, pissed off.

Romell Tukes

Chapter 27

MDC, Brooklyn

Ms. Dee had been rocking back and forth in her cell, thinking about her current situation. Being charged with three murders at her age, doing a prison bid wasn't in her plans.

"Lawyer visit, Ms. Dee, lawyer visit… last call," one of the female correctional officers yelled out on the intercom.

Hearing her name brought Ms. Dee outta her trance and back into reality. She jumped up, got dressed and grabbed her jail ID. The prison made inmates carry daily while walking the hallways.

Ms. Dee had been waiting to see a lawyer since being in jail, so she felt hope, wishing he or she could get her released.

Ten minutes later, Ms. Dee saw Mr. Goldenberg waiting for her at a door leading into a private room.

"Ms. Dee, correct?" asked Mr. Goldenberg in a new suit, looking at the folder in his hand.

"Yes, and who are you?"

"Well, I'm your lawyer and Jalisa's lawyer also." Mr. Goldenberg stepped in the room.

"I have no money for lawyers. Besides, you look like you're very expensive." Ms. Dee sat down, making him laugh.

"I'm paid in full, have no worries, you're in good hands."

"Hope so, will you be getting me out of here?" she asked.

"That's the goal," Mr. Goldenberg said, looking over her caseload he'd been studying.

"What do they have on me, and will my daughter be ok?"

"Let's focus on you right now. The DA is charging up with the two murders from over twenty years ago and the murder of a federal agent," the lawyer read the charges off a report.

"I never killed a federal cop." She looked shocked to hear this again.

"In the report it said you ran when Agent Hollis tried to arrest you. Once in the room, which is believed to be your bedroom, they said you pulled out an automatic weapon and started firing, hitting the agent in the neck as well as another officer. At the hospital, Agent Hollis was pronounced dead hours later from the gunshot wound." The lawyer took off his glasses, looking at Ms. Dee.

"I don't remember this, I'm getting old, I'm in my sixties." Ms. Dee tried to use the old card on him, but Mr. Goldenberg found it cute.

"We have to be honest with each other, Ms. Dee, or I won't fully be able to help you get out of here," he explained.

"What evidence do they have?"

"Enough to indict and charge you, Ms. Dee. The feds play dirty, but the only way you can really get outta this is if you give up some valuable info." He gave her an awkward pause.

"I'd rather die in jail."

"Ok, so ratting is out of the question because from the look of things, they really want your daughter."

"Well, I don't know nothing." Ms. Dee spoke with the lawyer for an hour longer before returning back to her unit.

***

White Plains, NY

Steel laid in the hospital bed with a butt pad resting under him, pissed off at the world for being shot up in the club. The doctors had a few more cat scans to run on Steel before he could leave, but people had been showing up to check on him daily, everybody from his girlfriend to his boys.

The night he got shot, Steel knew better than to make his way to any hospital in Queens, after a shooting in the area leaving victims dead.

He came out to White Plains and got treated without any police contacting or questioning him about his accident. The little niggas who shot him made his blood boil, but the only one he knew was King H.

"Yurro…." Montay walked into the room

"My boy, what's the vibes, my G," said Steel, happy to see his young boy.

Steel and Montay had a close relationship for some time now. Steel was the one who put the bag in Ice's ear about putting Montay on the team a while back.

"Niggas got you in the ass?"

"Yeah, when I find them, I'ma kill them niggas, word to my mother." Steel was mad, foaming out the mouth thinking about the scene.

"I heard bits and pieces of the story, but I heard shit got nasty, cuz."

"Facts, look at me, bro."

"What happened?"

"Niggas started fighting out the blue and I'm knocking niggas out left and right bro, on gang," Steel lied.

"Come on, cuz, this is me. I know you can't fight."

"Let me finish, bro."

"'light." Montay smirked.

"It's King H people, we rumbling with a gang of young niggas bro, then shots go off. You know me, I pull my shit out busting back, but niggas caught me lacking."

"Damn, bro."

"I'ma find King H."

"Son just came home days ago. I know boy official." Montay got Steel tighter.

"He a bitch. We gonna slide on all them Highbridge niggas and whoever he riding with."

"That's gonna spark some shit, but me and the boys got inside business." Montay thought about the shootout King H and he had in his hood.

"Fuck it, we ready."

"Facts. Let's show him who run the city, but I got ops on my side I need to get rid of, so it's lit." Montay thought about Body.

"We gonna slide on everybody," Steel said, not knowing Montay had beef with his own cousin.

Romell Tukes

Chapter 28

Uptown, The Bronx

Top was telling Body he had a lead on the ops. After digging up some info, Top was able to put two and two together about who Steel was, thanks to King H.

They were able to find out some more news about Steel through the grapevine, like who he worked for and who worked for him. When Top found out Montay was down with Steel and whoever the Ice nigga was, he got pissed off.

"I'm mad you weren't there, bro," said Top who had been talking about the club shooting for days.

"You said you did your research a second ago, so it's time to die." Body hated talking about shit, he just wanted to do shit.

"I can't believe Montay work with these niggas now, it's more litty. I always wondered who his plug was son, word to mother," Top said, driving up White Plains Road to see wild Jamaicans niggas out getting to a bag.

"Montay, what he have to do with this?" Body felt like he missed a peeped.

"That's the nigga people who got into it with bro, have you been listening to a word I been saying?" Top sucked his teeth, but he knew his friend had a lot of his mind.

The truth was, Body has been stressed lately thinking about his mom and grandma being in jail. His sister and little brother's well-being everything was too much at once. Two days ago, he spoke with the lawyer who said things aren't looking good, because the bail hearing on his mom and grandma were both denied.

"My bad, bro."

"A nigga named Steel. Son be in The South Bronx, he the nigga who got hit in the ass. I just found out his name. Steel works for some nigga name Ice nobody heard of, and our boy Montay slaves for them." Top saw the look on Body's face as he talked and knew it was priceless.

"That's my cousin and uncle."

"What?" Top hit the brakes hard at a stop sign.

"Nigga, Steel my cousin and Ice my uncle on my father's side." Body's mind was running crazy, because if he was at the club, he coulda stopped all this but it was a little too late, blood was drawn. Number one round to the streets, when blood is drawn, the beef will never end.

"This shit crazy, bro, so what we do now because all four niggas on go, hunting these niggas," Top said, wanting blood.

"Call it off."

"You bugging the fuck out," Top shouted, knowing Body lost his mind because the moment he put his guard down, he knew the niggas gonna slide on his people, especially a sneaky nigga like Montay.

"Bro, they're not regular ops, they're my family regardless, so let me have a sit down to see if we can avoid those odds." Body made sense to a point, but Top would never show a sign of weakness.

"I think it's dumb."

"We out here trying get money, not go to jail and die, bro." Body talking about money would open Top's eyes.

"I don't know, we can't trust them."

"Who says we trust? A game is meant to be played, so we just setting up limits."

"What if it backfires?"

"Then it's lit, bro. Them niggas only family by blood, you family by love." Body's words sat deep in Top's heart.

"Ok, set it up then for Pelham Park this weekend," Top suggested.

"Bet." Body pulled out his phone to call Ice, instead of Steel, who was a hothead.

***

Long Island, NY

Ice looked at his phone after just hanging up with his nephew, trying to figure out how he even got his number, and got mixed up in the drama.

"Baby, can we fuck some more before you leave? I won't see you for a few days," the sexy, brown-skinned woman Ice fucked once a week begged.

"Next time. I got shit to do, shawty, I don't play house," he told her before she climbed outta bed. She was built right with a nice firm ass that jiggled and was real.

"Ok, daddy."

Ice started to get dressed, first putting on his eighty-thousand-dollar Rolex watch, then his Cuban link chain worth two times more than the watch.

Ice couldn't believe it when Body called, requesting a sit down for the recent event that took place with Steel and him in the club. He didn't see his nephew in the spot tonight, so Ice figured Body must know somebody from the other side.

After the night he almost lost his life, he pushed the button to have all them little niggas killed. Now Steel was out the hospital, shit was about to hit the fan, but he agreed to meet with Body to see what his nephew had to say.

The last time he heard about Body was recently hearing about Jalisa's arrest. It was all over the news for days and Ice couldn't believe she was selling that much weight in Brooklyn.

Ice wondered if his brother Moss was alive, would shit be a lot different. When Moss died, Ice stopped checking up on his nephew and niece for years, caught up dealing with life and trying to chase a bag. He really hoped Body had nothing to do with Steel being shot, prayed he didn't have any dealings with the King H nigga, or shit could get real nasty.

Romell Tukes

Chapter 29

Pace University, NY

Brooklyn tried to focus on the lesson she was given, but her brain was clouded, reading the college textbook in her dorm study hall.

The thought of her mom and grandma being in prison didn't sit well with her. Every day she stressed the fact her mother was going through so much pain and tribulations in jail.

Speaking to Jalisa the other night brought an emotion over her she never could imagine. Brooklyn cried for days thinking about how quick a person's life can change for worse.

Brooklyn still didn't believe her mom was a drug dealer and she stood strong on that, because Jalisa taught her everything she knew about becoming a successful, independent business woman.

"Hey Brooklyn," Hope said, approaching the table with her arms full of books.

"Hope, what's up?" Brooklyn hadn't seen Hope in a few days, but on her *IG* social media page, Brooklyn saw Hope and Body together chilling.

"Come to look up some shit for class. I was with Body yesterday." Hope blushed thinking about Body, her soon-to-be boyfriend.

"I saw y'all on *IG*."

"Yeah, we vibing tight but he just be very busy."

"Trust me, I know that. Half the time he doesn't pick up."

"Oh, he does that to you also? Now I don't feel so sad," Hope replied.

At times when Body didn't pick up the phone, Hope would feel like he wasn't really into her, but now she understood that's who he was.

"I'm going back to my room, but I am calling you later." Brooklyn stood up to leave.

"Ok gurl, take it easy." Hope then went her way, ready to call it a night. She'd spend hours outta the day studying, working, and focusing on Body now because she was really feeling him.

Hope knew she could have any nigga she wanted, but there was something about Body she couldn't resist at all, and the way he treated her fucked up her head.

School had been going well for Hope she loved it and the thought of looking down the future meant a lot to her. The only thing missing outta her life was Body and she prayed soon he would open his eyes before it was too late.

***

Pelham Park, The Bronx

Steel couldn't believe his ears when Ice told him his little cousin Body knew the niggas who shot him. The meeting today had him on fire because he was already walking with Kane.

"I knew this nigga was up to something, bro," Steel said, hopping out of Ice's E-class 350 Mercedes-Benz.

"Why you assume that? He may not be up to shit, Body not built for the streets," Ice shot back, feeling the nice breeze.

"Jalisa in jail for moving weight, nobody had a clue. So, you think Body ain't got his hands in nothing?" Steel tried to make it make sense.

"You overthinking shit." Ice walked to the baseball field seeing people working out and jogging on the track.

"That's them niggas on the bleachers." Steel hated walking with a cane but the doctor said he had to until his ass cheek got better.

"Let me do all the talking, because you are still in your body, ready to talk crazy and shit." Ice knew Steel all too well, he would run his mouth all day.

"I hear you, son." Steel walked, twisting his whole lower body as if he was crippled with every step.

***

Body and Top saw Ice and Steel coming their way, so they both stood up. Top walked but he held his goofy side.

"Bro, be cool. I got this," said Body in a calm demeanor.

"I got my Glock on me." Top made sure he let Body know what type of time he was really on.

The main reason why Top told King H and Gage to hold their fire was because the ops were Body's real family, so he didn't want to put his best friend in any position where he had to choose sides.

"Little cuz, what's good?" Ice embraced Body with a pound.

"Same shit, how it's been?" Body shot back, seeing Steel face fight with Top.

"Ain't no need to speak on why we here, bro. Do you know these cats because they took one of ours and hit Steel up and I'm not happy." Ice made clear.

"They are my people and the shit that happened at the club did get outta hand on both parties from my understanding," Body replied.

"Nigga, you wasn't even there and when you became a street nigga?" Steel added, seeing Ice gave him a cold stare.

"Shut up," Ice told Steel. "I understand that, but blood was drawn, Body and somebody has to answer for it," Ice replied, looking dead in Top's face.

"I don't understand, bro." Body wanted to make sure he heard clearly.

I'ma make this quick and easy on you, son. Pick a side and whatever side you pick, it's no turning back," Ice stated.

"That's not hard, my nigga. I barely know you so I'm rock with my niggas," Body said strongly as Steel chuckled.

"You sure?" Ice asked.

"I'm positive, son, it's up from here I guess then," Body required, already knowing the cancer to it.

"I thought you were a little smarter, but I'll make sure they bury you respectfully," Ice stated.

"Same on my end," Body shot back, walking off.

"Call the goons?" Top asked.

"Let them know it's on and popping, G'z." Body was more than ready.

Romell Tukes

Chapter 30

Brooklyn, NY

Body finally took a free day to slide out to Brooklyn so he could see what his mom wanted him to get. Jalisa called him last night, informed him how her first court date went. The judge denied every motion Mr. Goldenberg put in on her behalf to get her released on bail and house arrest.

The DA wasn't playing any game, the Korean man wanted her to rot in prison. He made the note very clear to the courts with no mercy. "At the moment, I don't have a clue what I'm looking at, but it's not good," Jalisa explained being strong over the phone, but Body heard the fear in his mom's voice.

Driving down Church Avenue, he looked for the apartment building his mom gave him and quickly scoped it sitting on the corner. While parking his car, Hope called his cell phone.

"Hey ma, what's good." Body put her on FaceTime so he could see her beauty.

"What you doing?"

``Just got out of the shower, me and my homegirl are about to go grab a drink. You want to come?" she asked, hoping he would say yes, because she hadn't seen him in a few days and wanted some dick.

"I'm a little busy right now." Body got out on the dark Brooklyn street. To his surprise, the block was empty tonight, which was odd in Brooklyn because niggas be outside heavy.

"You always say that."

"It's true, ma, but I'ma make it up. Your birthday coming soon."

"Facts, and I'm trying to turn up."

"We will trust me."

"I miss you," she told him, blowing Body a kiss but he didn't give her a reply.

"Can I call you back in a few?" asked Body before the call failed and she hung up on him.

Body knew Hope was straight to catch feelings, but he had a lot going on, and giving his love to someone took a lot of time. He loved chilling with Hope and getting to know her, but his life was hacked. Body knew Hope would never understand because she wasn't in his shoes, nor was she a street bitch so he didn't waste time to explain.

Walking to the fifth floor, Body couldn't help but to play the guessing game with himself.

He found the key and let himself in the apartment to see nothing inside, except wood floors and white walls.

"What the fuck is that?" he mumbled to himself confused.

Body searched the back rooms then the bathrooms to find nothing whatsoever, except cleaning supplies. Then it hit him, the kitchen was where Jalisa told him to look. Inside the kitchen, Body opened the cabinets and oven to find a stack of bricks and money, wrapped up in tape.

"Oh shit." Body counted it. Jalisa had over a hundred kilos in the cabinets. Body saw garbage bags in the bathroom, so he went to collect a couple and started tossing everything in the bags.

He made two trips to his car, excited about his future plans because Top had just told him they need a plug, but Body thought that was too dangerous.

Now the crew would be good for a while, but Body came up with a plan to put half the drugs and money up for a rainy day. All the paper Top had brought him, he needed to find a safer place than there, because Mickey lived with him now so Body wanted to move smarter.

***

Lower Eastside, NY

Papa had a condo in Manhattan on the top floor, he stayed from time to time whenever he wanted a good view of the city's night lights.

Looking over the city, he thought about his childhood and brother. Coming to the states was a blessing for him overall because he found a way for his family.

Tomorrow, he had another sit down with Mark to go over business plans. Papa found out through a close friend of Mojoa's that a woman came to Miami to purchase a large amount of drugs from Mojoa, but he didn't have a name for Papa.

Ice needed more drugs also, before Papa went out to L.A. tomorrow for the sit down with Mark.

"You ok, baby? Why are you out here alone?" Papa's beautiful girlfriend was tying her robe, walking up behind him as he stood on a small terrace.

"Go back to sleep, love." Papa loved his girlfriend, she was the best thing that happened to him since his ex-wife, who now truly hated him. Papa was married to a beautiful Colombian woman for over ten years. The love they shared was so rare, the two got married their first week of meeting each other.

Papa knew for a long time she was the only one, but things went for a crazy left turn when Papa started to use drugs. Papa did some hurtful things that took his wife away from him, but he prayed one day she'd be able to come back, and her replacement was the perfect fit.

'I'm just checking on you."

"That's why I love you, my dear," Papa said, kissing her soft lips and gripping her big ass.

"Love you too, Papa."

"Tomorrow you wanna come to L.A.?" he asked.

"To shop?"

"Yes, of course, baby. I know how you love Christian Dior and Chanel."

"Yep, can't wait, Papa." his girlfriend Cyn said, kissing his lips before walking off smiling.

Romell Tukes

Chapter 31

Bogota, Colombia

Mark loved to travel, especially to beautiful places like Colombia, because the weather was always nice. The women all had natural beauty and amazing bodies. Last night he had five sexy ladies in his company at the fancy resort he was staying in.

Every time he would come out to Colombia, Mark always stayed at the same resort, because they treated him like the king he was.

A car trailed behind two bulletproof SUVs on the way to pay El Bien a visit from the man who put Mark in the game when he was just a young man. Mark had a lot of respect for the older gentleman who treated Mark like his own son.

El Bien lived in the city because he loved the view, so he owned five condo buildings right next to the crystal-clear beach his wife loved.

Mark's personal driver pulled into the lower garage area, so they could take the elevator upstairs to the penthouse. El Bien was always protected and surrounded by teams of security guards. Being one of the biggest drug lords in Colombia, El Bein had to stay protected at all times, especially dealing with his enemy, which is his family.

Decades ago, El Bien's brothers and sister all fell out over money and started their own cartel families. It didn't take long before a big family war broke out across Colombia, leaving dead bodies piled up all over the place.

Papa ended up marrying one of El Bien sisters and moving her to the states while she still controlled a cartel in Colombia. The marriage lasted a long time, but shit got crazy, and they separated after ten years.

In the elevator, he turned off his phone as a sign of respect for his boss. Inside the large condo with the high ceilings, guards were posted everywhere. They led Mark to the outside terrace, which was spacious, with a mini bar and two tables with chairs.

"Mark." El Bien's English was better than a lot of people from the states because he studied it and lived in L.A. back and forth.

"I was in L.A. the other day with Papa,'' said Mark, taking a seat as a naked Colombian woman with big breasts brought him a drink of clear liquid.

"Good ole Papa. I head what happened to Mojoa, that's bad business." El Bien had a history with Papa through his sister, whom Papa had married.

"Yeah, we trying to figure out who killed him now."

"Don't bust your brain, Mark. He was a piece of shit, Mojoa had it coming."

"That was my investment."

"Anytime you invest, you're taking a risk in losing, that's the game," El Bien said as he offered Mark a cigar and lit one for himself.

"I agree, but how's things going out here?"

"The government is starting to get on my nerves. They have been knocking my loads, Mark. This is why the last two shipments had to be sent out in little amounts," El Bien stated, knowing Mark's real reason for being here today.

"That's why my work been stepped on and cut over hundred times by the time it reached me?"

"Yes, but I can promise you I'ma make it up, Mark. You do good business, but I had to do that," El Bien explained.

"Not to me."

"Yes, to you and everybody else, but I recently got one of the government officials in my pocket, so now I have a new way to get the drugs out to you."

"Great news, when can I be expecting the arrival?" Mark seemed excited.

"Next week."

Mark was happy with the reply, so he changed the conversation and talked about the good old times.

***

42nd St, NYC

Ray got off the train at Grand Central Station and looked at all the people around him in his Army uniform. Ray had a week and a half to spend with his family before they shipped him to Iran in the Middle East.

Rocking his Army outfit, in shape with a low cut, Ray felt like a true soldier. He'd been so caught up with training and focusing on going overseas, he'd lost the contract of his friends and family.

Body was supposed to be out front waiting for him, he couldn't wait to see his boys. He wondered what they were doing with their lives. He knew Body would be in college or working a good job because he also was smart, but Top was a different story.

Outside, Body was double-parked in front of a blue cab when he got out the Charger, Ray approached him.

"My fucking boy." Ray gave him a hug.

"Damn, my nigga, you really look like *Major Payne* and your weight up." Body couldn't believe how big Ray got in a short amount of time.

"I work out from five am to eight am every morning." Ray got inside the car, tossing his bag in the back, liking the interior of the car.

"This a good look, bro, glad you home but shit nasty out here."

"I'm here for nine days, but what's going on?" Ray seemed surprised because from the look of shit, life was good for Body.

"My mom and g mom in prison, Montay and my cousin at war with us, and niggas killed King H mom last night so he going crazy," Body said jumping on the traffic-jammed highway leading back to The Bronx.

"Wow, bro. I don't even know what to say, son." Ray didn't even want to ask what Jalisa was in jail for, or when his boy King H got out, Ray just said a silent prayer for his crew.

Romell Tukes

Chapter 32

Jackson PJ's, The Bronx

Montay and Steel posted up in the building's lobby, surrounded by goons on a late-night drinking, smoking, and regular dice games took place every night. Steel's young boys made so much noise, the neighborhood police didn't even bother to show up anymore when the residence called.

"That was a brilliant move, Montay, you shoulda seen that bitch's face when niggas caught that bitch coming out of the gas station in Highbridge." Steel laughed, referring to the murder of King H's mom a few days ago.

Montay knew where King H's mom lived because she lived on the same block as Montay's ex-girlfriend. It wasn't hard to put a plan together to send their ops a message.

"Facts bro, but I can't believe Body is in the middle of the shit." Montay knew Top and Body were best friends, but he had no clue he fucked with King H or cared that he was related to his plug and peoples.

"Fuck that little nigga, he chose his friends over family so that's how it is, bro." Steel strongly considered Body a sworn enemy now.

"I wonder who this weird nigga Top getting all this work from, because my homie Uptown said he just hit some nigga from White Plains Road with a few keyz." Montay knew Top to be a robber, not a drug dealer.

"We gonna figure it all out, but first we need to spin on these niggas until they get dizzy."

"Say that, son. I got the little homies on it as we speak," Montay assured him as the niggas started to argue with one of Steel boys over a bad roll on the dice game.

***

Highbridge, The Bronx

King H hadn't left his apartment since his mom's death, he refused to open the door, answer his phone or talk to anybody.

Tonight, would have been his mom's birthday, so he was really feeling it as he sipped on his second gallon of Henny in two days. He looked out his window, to see it was dark outside with a half moon.

King H took one more sip of Henny and put on a black Champion hoodie before grabbing two loaded pistols he had on his coffee table. Leaving the apartment, he thought about a plan that would ease his mind a little so he could have a peaceful sleep.

***

Castle Hill PJ's, The Bronx

The trap wasn't doing too good tonight, but niggas was still out trying to make a dollar outta nothing.

Maine and Uno were block huggers, they would post up rain, summer and snow, trying to get money. Maine was Montay's older brother, who was in a wheelchair after a drive-by took his legs out ten years ago on the same block he hustled on.

Uno was his loud cousin, known for shooting niggas on sight, he had a vicious name through the Castle Hill area.

"I'm ready to go inside, bro," said Maine, seeing the hood was dead.

"We the only niggas out son," Uno shot back, sitting on the benches in the front of his building.

"Facts. Push me to the store so I can buy a Newport." Maine grabbed the wheels on his chair, turning around and preparing to roll up the block.

"What you think about this shit going on with Top and dem niggas?" Uno asked Maine, pushing him to the corner store on this nice night, looking up to see a half-moon up close.

"Top ain't the type niggas wanna sleep on son, word to mother. I respect the young boy's gun game." Maine gave respect when it was due, and Top earned it.

"Word on the street is his friend Body really be crushing shit, my G." Uno pushed Maine in the store that was open twenty-four seven in the hood.

"I don't know, son."

"Boy moves like a ghost. Shit, come to think about it, I never saw son." Uno only heard of Body but couldn't put a face to the killer.

"Grab me some Cheetos, cuz." Maine couldn't reach the Hot Flames Cheetos, so Uno got it for him and paid for the snacks and a pack of Newports.

"What's up with that white girl you had coming though with the phat ass, bro?" Uno asked, stepping outside to see a nigga rocking a hoodie but barely showing his face.

"Man, she for the gang, but she not trying let me fuck. The bitch let me eat her pussy twice and lick her ass. That was it, bro." Maine shook his head.

"No homo, but I ain't know your shit get up, boy," Uno stated as Maine gave him a cold look.

"What type of time you on, my nigga? Just because I'm in a wheelchair don't mean shit. All she gotta do is pick me up," Maine said, making Uno cry laughing.

"Yurrooooo, pardon me, fam. Y'all got a light," the man with the hoodie who was posted up at the store stated, following them.

"Nah fam, we don't smoke," Uno said not falling for the lighter trick, because he saw a lot of niggas get their faces cut when they reached for the lighter.

The hoodie man saw a pack of cigs in Maine's lap and smirked before smoothly pulling out a handgun.

BOC....

BOC....

BOC....

BOC....

BOC....

BOC....

BOC....

BOC....

BOC....

Uno's body collapsed on the ground and Maine tried to roll way, but King H grabbed the wheelchair and flipped him out of it. King H stood over Maine and emptied the clip in Maine's head, killing him completely.

Chapter 33

Castle Hill, The Bronx

Montay entered his mom's building thinking about the news of his brother Maine. He couldn't believe he was dead. Killing a nigga in a wheelchair was the lowest of all lows, but Montay knew in beef, anything was open for kill.

His mom normally called him once a day, but knowing what happened to Maine last night, she most likely had an emotional breakdown. On his mom's floor, he used the spare key, thinking which nigga from Top's crew murdered his brother, so he could strike back ten times harder.

"Mom, where you at?" asked Montay, knowing his mom was normally in the kitchen or living room, watching TV because she couldn't do too much moving, due to her weight. Since he was a kid, Montay's mom had been a plus size woman but now she weighted close to four hundred pounds.

Montay saw his mom sitting in a chair with a crown on her head, the one from the 18th century the kings used to wear. He laughed, walking in front of the chair wondering why she was still silent, but his mom played a lot of games.

When he got a full look at his face Montay heart almost skipped a bear as he saw the two bullet holes in his mom's head with a red flag tied around her neck.

Tears started to build in Montay's eyes, looking at the way someone killed her with no remorse. Staring at the crown and the red flag, Montay figured out who took his mama's life, the bitch ass nigga King H. Montay knew something would eventually happen after killing King H's mom. Thinking more into it, he was able to match Maine's death to King H also. He must have done all the killing last night.

Not knowing what to do, Montay called 911 and reported the gruesome scene, then waited for the officials to arrive. Just looking at his deceased mother crushed his heart. He wanted to kill any and everybody close to King H.

Montay just lost two people close to him in a matter of twenty-four hours. He needed some get back, but first he had to heal from the losses.

Chapter 34

MDC, Brooklyn

Jalisa peeped at the C.O. in the elevator with her staring at her up and down sexually, but Jalisa had other shit going on than to be concerned with a lame ass guard.

"You too pretty to be in jail," the tall male officer said, escorting Jalisa back to her floor.

"Thanks."

"I'm working your block next week." He gave her a look.

"So, what... you want a cookie?" Jalisa knew what he was getting at, because the lame guards would fuck the female inmates in slop closets or in their cells.

"I just wanna taste your cookie," he shot back smiling.

"Maybe when I'm dead." She got off the elevator walking into her unit, thinking about her court day.

Jalisa went straight to her cell, not trying to talk with anybody plus half of the nosey bitches on the block was ratting anyway.

"Hey celly," Marylean said as she looked up from reading a book, taking off her reading glasses.

Marylean became her cellmate days ago when she arrived from the prison in Florida, to give some time back on her appeal she recently won. Marylean was in her mid-forties but looked twenty, everything about her was beautiful from the way she looked, talked and walked. Being a hundred percent Colombian, with a nice body she kept toned through exercise, Marylean would give any bitch in the jail a run for their money.

"Hey, girl." Jalisa sat down in the green plastic chair all the inmates had inside their cells.

"How was the court?" Marylean didn't know too much about Jalisa's case besides she had a big case including queen pin status.

"It sucked. They have nothing on me." Jalisa tried to hold back her frustration, but she was so upset

Talking about the case to people in the unit was a big no because inmates soul jumped on people's cases. The first time Jalisa heard the term jumping on someone's case, she was confused until she'd seen it happen with her own eyes. A young woman named Beka told her celly Dawn everything about her case and about a murder she and some guy did. Two weeks later, Dawn disappeared and Beka was hit with six more new charges, thanks to Dawn snitching to her lawyer and the DA for time out.

"They offer you anything?"

"Not nothing I'm taking, sixty-five years is a long time," Jalisa complained.

"Shit girl, I'm trying to get that now. Anything is better than life, plus two hundred fifty-six years," Marylean stated.

"I know." Jalisa kept forgetting how long Marylean got for murders and drug trafficking.

"You gonna be ok? I'ma go grab our chow. I'm hungry."

"Ok." Jalisa sat there thinking about her mom's court date tomorrow and what they were gonna do with her.

Chapter 35

Manhattan, NY

Body needed a small getaway to clear his mind, so he brought Hope out to a nice fancy hotel, overlooking the city lights from the balcony. Spending time with Hope was something he had been meaning to do but he had a lot going on.

King H was wilding, trying to kill everything connected to Montay, not giving a fuck if he got caught or not. Body knew one person could bring down a whole Army, so he'd tried to install this into King H's hardheaded brain.

Even though Top and Gage's main focus was the bag, they both were focused on the beef as well, because nobody knew how Ice, Steel, or Montay were coming. They were all very connected.

"Let me take your mind off of whatever you're going through." Hope appeared from inside, wearing a robe with a sexy G-string on underneath, already knowing tonight was the big night.

"I don't know if you can take my mind off what's really going on, well maybe for a second." He looked her in the eyes as she handed him a glass of Mo to drink.

"Try me, Body."

"My mom and grandma are locked up; little brother and sister is emotionally fucked up. I'm going through shit out here you couldn't imagine. Picture your own family, people you looked up to, trying to kill you over nothing," he explained.

"Everything God is putting you through is only to make you stronger." She tried to find the right words to make him feel good but deep down, she knew Body needed more than good words.

"Sounds nice, Hope, but don't let this nice guy act fool you."

"I'm not, trust me. I know a real nigga when I see one, but none of that street shit matters to me."

"Oh nah," Body replied now holding her around her slim waist, standing face-to-face with Hope.

"Nope, because I know you have a good heart that's screaming to be loved." She touched his chest, tracing his heart with her long pink manicured nails.

"You sure?"

"Yes, and I want to be the one to love it." She looked him in his could eyes and felt his connection as they kissed.

Body slid a finger into her drenched coochie, which was super tight.

"Hmmmmm…" she moaned as he picked her up, carrying her to the master bedroom with the mirrored ceiling.

"This is what you want?" Body whispered in her ear, laying Hope down.

"Yes, for life," she replied as he got undressed and climbed between her legs, entering he love box. Hope's pussy was so wet, Body felt like he was in a slip and slide contest.

Body slow stroked then long stroked her, hitting her bottom while Hope's intact walls gripped the life outta his penis.

"Damn babe," Body managed to say, feeling his build up about to explode in her love ocean. Body brought condoms but he forgot all about them and had to focus on the moment.

"Ohhhh shit, yess… fuck me harder," Hope moaned, gripping the bed sheets about to bite her bottom lip off.

Body and Hope went at it all night, with one break in between the whole fuck session.

***

Spanish Harlem, NY

Top picked up his boy Curt, a Spanish nigga in the same set as him he met on Rikers Island years ago on the minor block in building four on C74 where shit was turned up.

"You that boy, I got a mean strain for us, you heard," Curt said smoking a blunt of weed on parole. Curt felt like since weed was legal now, he could smoke it all day on papers are not.

"I fell back from the licks, *skrap*. I'm on a different type of time." Top didn't tell Curt he's moving keys because he knew the man type a jack boy just like him.

"Nah son, this nigga is the plug I heard he be moving like five hundred kilos just through Spanish Harlem alone," Curt said, now catching Top's attention.

"Nigga, nobody moving them type of bird out here," Top replied, looking at Curt's face for truthfulness.

"I swear on the set, this nigga got a small restaurant a few blocks up he used as a stash spot," Curt explained.

"Let's go right now, you know where the drugs at?" Top tried to bluff him.

"Yes, in the basement."

"How do you know all this shit anyway, bro?" Top had to ask because he wondered, *if Curt knows so much about the stain, how come he ain't been robbed the spot?*

"A bitch from my block works there so she put me on. So, I called you because I know how you give it up," Curt pumped him up.

"I'ma look into it first because it seems too easy."

"Nah, buzzing shit real."

"Facts of life." Top drove around smoking good weed, thinking about everything Curt was spitting.

"Whenever you are ready, it's no rush, but tomorrow is the night. They got the drugs because they close early," Curt said, sounding like a professional thief.

"You've been doing your homework I see, bro. I am back tomorrow at the same time, be ready. And Curt, you better not be capping," Top said before dropping him off.

Romell Tukes

Chapter 36

MDC, Brooklyn

Body came to see his mom in jail at the Federal Pretrial Building, a place he was starting to hate. Today he tried to get his mom and grandma pulled down on a visit, but for some strange reason, his granny had denied the visit.

Brooklyn was eager to come today when he told her about today's visit, but Jalisa begged him not to bring her up until she was mentally ready. Body tried to contact the lawyer a few days ago, but his assistant informed him Mr. Goldenberg was fighting a murder in the Eastern District of New York.

Waiting on Jalisa seemed like forever, but that gave him all the time to pre-meditate what to say. He still couldn't believe his mom is in prison and was a queen pin, but there were times when he was growing up, she would leave the house at all hours of the night.

Jalisa walked out just as his mind had started to shift over to Ray's birthday today. Body wanted to take him out to eat and surprise his friend with a new car. Even though Ray made it clear he wanted nothing to do with Body's lifestyle, their friendship would forever remain strong and health. Ray was supposed to be going back to the Army tomorrow, so Body couldn't wait to surprise him with a new Chevy truck.

"Hey, my handsome son." Jalisa sat down with bags under her eyes and a fresh streak of gray hair clearly visible. Body disliked seeing his mom like that, but she kept a warm smile on her face.

"How have you been, my queen?"

"Hang in there, my young king, I heard you got a little princess you been seeing." Jalisa gave him an "I know it all" look.

"Her name is Hope. She went to school with me. I was gonna tell you once we got serious and we are now." Body knew better than to tell his big mouth sister anything.

"Make sure you treat her right most men these day don't know how to treat a young woman or a woman because they never saw nobody treat their mothers correctly. So, they grow up not knowing how to treat females. Most people only go off what they see, not the morals of life," Jalisa explained, schooling her son on how to be a real man like his father.

"That makes sense."

"I know it does. For example, your father treated every woman with the utmost respect. That was why I had to beat a lot of bitches up, to keep them off him." Jalisa laughed.

Body barely talked about his dad because he was mad Moss wasn't here to teach him certain things in life. The small shit like how to play basketball, helping with homework, or how to drive. He still respected his dad's name and all he did for his family. Jalisa told him stories all the time about how Moss created a legacy.

"Have you been to court?" Body changed the subject and saw how his mom's smile turned into a sad face.

"I start trial in two months."

"Trial?" He was confused, knowing it wouldn't be good.

"Yes, they tried to offer me sixty-five." Her face saddened.

"65 days you should of took that, Mommy."

"No Body 65 years" she saw him almost choked on his own saliva.

"This can't be real," Body said to himself.

"Trust me it is, but don't worry. I just need you to hold the family together. You never know what God got planned," she said putting on a fake smile, knowing the odds were against her.

"I'ma hold it down, Mom. Facts. I went to that spot in Brooklyn and that should hold shit over until I find someone to deal with," Body spoke in code about a drug connect.

"Be careful, son. My plug was recently killed in Miami. I was starting to think someone was after me. Mojoa was a good person, just a whole Mexican." She laughed to herself, seeing Body gaze off. "You ok, baby?" she asked.

"Mojoa? Mom, he was your plug?"

"Yes, you heard of him?" She saw his concern

Body lowered his voice. "I killed him." Jalisa looked at him with a stern look, thinking he was lying, until she saw the same look Moss used to have.

"Fuck… you need to leave the state. He is very connected. If word gets out you did it, Body, your life will be in danger." She got scared for the first time, because she saw how Mojoa got people's whole families killed in different states recently.

"Mom, I'm good, trust me. I got a team and we all on go time."

"It's not about that, son."

"Trust me, Mom, please. I'm good." He saw her ease up a little.

"Someone paid for his life?" she asked.

"Yes, a woman named Cyn." Body had never disclosed information about any of his clients before today.

"I never heard of her but be careful please." She rubbed his soft face before their visit was ended. Body left the jail thinking how small the world was and wondering who the fuck was this Cyn woman.

***

Spanish Harlem, NY

Curt had been talking Top's ear off for a whole thirty minutes, and he didn't hear a word he said besides kilos over and over. Top just wanted to get the job done so he could chill with Ray for his birthday and before he went back to the Army.

"Fam, please shut up, you 're giving me a headache," Top said looking at the small Spanish restaurant prepare their last customer food bag before closing.

"Damn son, my bad. I was just telling you about the last lick I did with Scooter and Riggs," Curt said in the driver seat of his rental.

"Let's go, son leaving." Top hopped out once he saw the last customer leave. He rushed across the street, leaving Curt behind trying to catch the door. Top made it inside to see three beautiful women cleaning, all of them Dominican.

"Get down and nobody gets hurt. Yo, where is the stash at?" Top asked, already knowing.

The women pointed down to the basement, quickly seeing Curt enter with the man she fucked from time to time, when he had his bag up. Top grabbed the woman and forced her downstairs into the basement leading the way.

Downstairs, there were dusty boxes and tables everywhere, plus it was dark. Top saw a movement ahead and before he could sight his target, the shooter fired three shots hitting the women in front of him.

Boc....

Boc....

Boc....

Boc....

Boc....

Boc....

Top and Curt fired back, hitting the gunman in his chest dropping him on boxes. Top rushed over to the other old Spanish man breathing, trying to stay alive.

"Where are the drugs and money?" Top asked, standing over the man with a gun pointed to his face as Curt checked the basement area.

"Papa moved everything two nights ago and left twenty thousand. He took it all too. Check the cooler, I swear," the Spanish man took his last breath, but it didn't stop Top from finishing him.

BOC....

BOC....

Top put two in his skull, then looked for the cooler which he located in the far back.

"They got us," Top called Curt to show him the stack of frozen money, which looked like twenty grand, but no drugs.

"Damn son, my bad, we late. Dude musta been on to niggas." Curt was tight he lost the big time come up, but as he reached for the money, Top cut him short.

"Slow it down, champ, this one is on you." Top got the money for himself.

"It's like that? I didn't get nothing, Blood?" Curt was furious.

"I got something for you." Top fired three bullets in Curt's dome, killing him. Top left out the basement unaware the cameras caught his every move.

Romell Tukes

Chapter 37

Uptown, The Bronx

The night was still young, so Body wanted to take Ray out to have a drink at a new hookah lounge near White Plains Road he was hearing about. Body had never been a club fiend, but he didn't mind stepping out every once in a blue moon.

"That food got me feeling fat, bro. I'm glad I came back home and I can't front, I be missing y'all," Ray stated, feeling tipsy from the drink he had at BBQ's in Bay Plaza.

"I'm proud of you, my nigga, we out here in the field risking our lives for dumb shit and you made a way."

"I mean, I'm in the field too, this just a different type of field, bro. I never saw a seven-year-old kid hold an AK-47 with no fear if he kills you or dies." Ray went on a month's tour in Iran, just for training and saw some scary shit that haunted him at night.

"No cap, bro. I would have shot the shit out his little ass." Body laughed, pulling into the gas station to get wraps for his weed and gas.

"I was thinking about it," Ray admitted as Body went into a store to pay for his items, texting Top where they were on their way to.

Coming out the store, an all-black Track Hawk pulled into the gas station with a loud scream, rolling down its windows. Body saw Steel and Montay hanging out the windows with a TEC-9 and a MAC-11 spraying shit up, trying to hit Body as he jumped on the ground.

TAT....
TAT....
TAT....
TAT....
TAT....
TAT....
TAT....

TAT....

TAT....

TAT....

TAT....

TAT....

Body crawled to a garbage can until the Track Hawk peeled out the lot. He jumped up to check on Ray, rushing to open the passenger door. He almost cried when Ray's lifeless body slowly fell out of the car.

Ray had bullet holes in his head, face, ear, neck, upper torso and his cheeks. Twenty-one rounds hit Ray, he didn't see the setup, while playing *Call of Duty* on his iPhone.

Police sirens sound like they were close, so Body lifted the bar after taking his gun out. Leaving Ray was the hardest thing he had to do, but his boy was dead, there was nothing he or the police could do about it.

***

City Island, The Bronx

Three Days Later

Cyn loved the smell of fresh cooked food, especially seafood, which was her favorite. This was why she would come down to City Island as frequently as possible. She sat on the outside deck waiting on Body to arrive.

This morning she called him, and he played dumb so well, as if he didn't know her. Cyn started to think it was the wrong number. When she told him the code, 12A4401, he then told Cyn to meet him somewhere in City Island, which was perfect because she was starving.

Most people would assume Cyn was just a beautiful face with a nice body, but if they only knew the real Cyn. Growing up in poverty deep in the slums of Puerto Rico, life wasn't meant to be successful. When her mom died, Cyn along with her baby sister and brother, met their father, a rich drug connect who did business with the Mexican Cartel, moving heavy weight into the states from Miami to L.A.

Everything was good, until one day Cyn came home from private school, to see their father laying on the floor with his heart cut out. The Mexican Cartel double crossed Cyn's father once they found a better way to get their drugs in and out the states.

Moving to New York with family, Cyn got adapted to the fast shady lifestyle and started rolling with big time dope boys early in her life, ever since she was nineteen. Once she met Papa, he took good care of Cyn and spoiled the shit outta her. Even though he met Cyn when he was married, things got serious once Papa broke up with his wife, for many reasons Cyn didn't give a fuck about.

Looking over her shoulder, Body was stepping towards the table in a nice Dior outfit with limited edition sneakers Dior only made ten of.

"Nice attire," she said.

"Thanks." Body's voice was flat, he still was hurt over Ray's death. Today was his first time leaving the crib, except to pick up Mickey from the bus stop, because he had summer school four days a week.

"Why do you look so sad?" she questioned, seeing he wasn't in the right mind set.

"That's none of your concern."

"Fair."

"What can I help you with?"

"Straight to the point. I like your style, Body," Cyn said, pulling out a yellow folder from her Louis Vuitton bag, handing it to him under the table just in case there were eyes somewhere.

"What's this?" He opened it to see a photo of an older man with a few addresses underneath the picture.

"Your next mission." She smiled.

"I got a lot going on right now, I'll pass." Body handed her back the folder.

"Look, I am a businesswoman who needs this job done. I'll pay a half-million up front," she begged.

"It's not about the money."

"After this, I won't ask you for nothing else, and I'll do you a big favor." Cyn smirked.

"What's that? Because I'm sure whatever it is, I'm not buying it." Body saw Cyn lean to whisper something in his ear which raised his eyebrows.

"Ok, deal. When your part is done, I'll handle mines, and send my money." Body took the folder and left as Cyn watched him walk away, eating her fish and shrimp.

Chapter 38

Burnside, BX

Gage threw a small cookout in his auntie's back yard for his three-year-old son's birthday party. There were a bunch of kids and grownups having fun on the nice summer day. The kids played in the pool Gage had bought while he took control of the grill cooking everything, from hot dogs and chicken wings to hamburgers.

"Where dat Henny at, cuz?" Top said, coming out back with King H, checking his surroundings and making sure no ops was lurking.

"Bro, it's all kids and old people out here, you can chill the fuck out," Gage told King H, who was looking crazy.

"Just got to make sure because kids killing shit too these days." King H's remark made Top and Gage stare at him at the same time.

Since King H's mom died, they knew he'd been a little off mentally. But both men knew how it felt to take a loss or two, but King H had been getting the worst of luck back-to-back.

"This weekend, I gotta bury Ray. This shit starting to get the best of me," Top said, snatching Gage gallon of Henny from the table in front of them.

"It's ok, trust and believe, blood will be delivered real soon," King H added with a deep voice.

"You good, bro? You been acting weird lately," Gage asked, looking at King H's dark eyes.

"The earth weighs the judgment of a man, and the sun makes the choices we have no control over. Every time blood is drawn, it sinks into the ground like a sponge, but the blood from our enemy still stains the surface of this place we all live. I have to go, farewell my kings," said King H, leaving the party as Gage and Top stood there, each lost in their own thoughts.

"What the fuck was that all about?" Top broke the ice.

"I don't know but you think we should get some help?" Gage asked seriously, because he knew one nigga from the hood who used to talk to crazy shit, just like King H just did and one day, the dude spazzed out and lit up seven people in a Target parking lot.

"You mean like mental help?"

"Yes."

"Nah, the homie will be ok, he just venting. A few more bodies under his belt, he'll be okay." Top and Gage shared a laugh while grilling, smoking, and drinking.

***

White Plains, NY

Days Later

Body couldn't bring himself to go see Ray get carried yesterday because he felt like his friend would still be alive if it was for him. The guilt he carried was far worse than being stabbed or shot. Brooklyn wants to meet the Cheesecake Factory, which was also a nice restaurant with good food.

Mickey came along but Body let him go to the game section until he's ready to sit and eat. This was about the only family time Body had in months, maybe since the Miami trip a couple of months ago.

Brooklyn sat in the booth section, looking cute wearing make-up, with her hair twisted up in box braids.

"What's up, sis?" Body gave her a strong tight hug and she gave one back.

"You losing weight." She looked him up and down.

"Damn, I don't get a hey."

"Hey skinny," she joked, sitting back down.

"Skinny is in these days."

"What? Boy bye. I need me a nigga with muscles, you bugging. I am following this guy on social media named Romell the Trainer on *IG*. He got a workout group called Muscle Fit Gang, maybe you'd could join," Brooklyn roasted her brother.

"You got dem jokes today, huh? You better return that lion hair before he come get your ass, and I told you about using that Gorilla Glue to tape on the edges." Body had her dying in laughs as she patted her blonde weave, loving it.

"I paid for it, nigga."

"How's school?" Body got serious, but he loved how they would always share laughs the hardest of times.

"Good, I been studying, trying to stay focused and happy at the same time."

"Me too, sis. When the last time you spoke to Mommy?" Body didn't want to be the one to tell Brooklyn about the offer Jalisa got or the trial. He'd rather their mom tell her because Brooklyn was very emotional.

"Last night."

"What did she say?"

"Nigga don't play. You went to see her, so you already know about the offer they gave her and the trial shit." Brooklyn sounded crushed, but she'd been holding on.

"Yeah, but it's gonna all work out, we just gotta have faith."

"I keep telling myself that, but I'm sorry for what happened to Ray. I liked him and I heard he was doing good in the Army. I don't know why people always come back to the place that held them back or tried to kill their dreams." Brooklyn shook her head.

"Only God knows."

"Brooklynnnnnn," Mickey yelled, jumping in his sister's lap like a little kid, but he was too heavy.

"Hi, big boy, sis miss you." Brooklyn loved her little brother to death. She really had to go through the same thing they did with losing Jalisa and Ms. Dee to the prison system.

They spent the whole night together, going out to movies in White Plains, having a blast around each other.

Romell Tukes

Chapter 39

Manhattan, NY

It's 2:30 am and Ice woke up out his sleep to a text message from Papa, informing him about an emergency sit down on 37th Street in a private garage. At first, Ice tried to ignore the text, but he forgot about his product Papa had, so he figured the meeting had to be concerning his brother.

The drugs were moving slow in The Bronx but his team in Harlem been picking up the slack so delay right now on product would fuck up what he had going on right now.

He let Steel and Montay handle the beef with Body and his little crews, but it was starting to affect his money. Word on the street is Top moving weight all through The Bronx from west to south. Yesterday, Ice yelled at Steel because Body and his boys were all still breathing and alive, not to mention, fucking up Ice's income.

Ice knew Moss would be turning in his grave right now if he found out Ice was trying to kill him. Moss taught Ice the game, but never told him about the double cross drawing family blood for a green piece of paper but that was something the streets taught him.

The garage was on the right, next to a skyrise building. Ice hoped he didn't have to pay for parking because he wasn't planning on staying long away.

A gray and white two-tone Rolls Royce Wraith was parked in the back corner surrounded by parked cars, all residents of the complex. Ice saw Papa's name on the front license plate and he saw Papa's headlights on, so he parked next to the wall and left his car running, hoping to be in and out.

Ice opened the unlock passenger door to see nobody was inside. "What the fuck?" Ice mumbled, not in the mood for games.

The second Ice turned around a long nose barrel was pointed directly at his face.

"Right on time," the woman said with grin.

"Who the fuck are you?" Ice never saw the woman a day in his life he started to wonder if Papa set him up.

"Do I really have to explain? I'm not too heavy on patience," she shot back, looking at her lady Rolex watch.

"That's the least you can do since Papa sent you." Ice was trying to fish and think of a way outta the situation.

"Ok, I guess it can be your last wish. A good friend of mines wants you dead, but he got a lot on his plate so for hm to help me, I had to help him. You get me?"

"Not really, how does Papa fall into this? You texted me from his number."

"Papa sleep. I made sure I fucked him good and added sleeping pills to his drinks, my boo gonna be out for a while. I knew you worked for Papa, so this was too easy" she giggled.

"Who's your friend?"

"You ask a lot of questions, but this can be your last one," she said.

BOOM....

BOOM....

BOOM....

BOOM....

Cyn shot Ice in his face, seeing blood splatter on the roof of Papa's Wraith as Ice's body fell to the floor, landing at Cyn's feet.

I know there is a twenty-four-hour car wash around here, Cyn thought, climbing in the car and pulling off, listening to the *Hot 97* radio station.

***

North Hampton, L.I.

Next Day

Papa drove his Wraith to meet up with Mark at his mansion. Today, Papa felt overly tired for some reason but last night, Cyn gave him the best oral sex he had in a long time. This coming weekend, Papa wanted to have a threesome, something he and Cyn did on the regular.

Pulling into Mark's gated community, he saw a small red dot on his mat.

"How the fuck I get catch up there, Cyn?" Papa stated to himself as a third person, before seeing Mark's nice home.

Mark stepped out front to welcome his guest of honor as he always did.

"My best friend," said Mark, giving Papa a hug.

"I'm only your best friend when someone has to die," Papa said, walking into the breathtaking home.

"Cheer up, my friend, you think you know me so well, come out to the courtyard." Mark patted Papa on the shoulder.

"How's the wife, Mark? I haven't seen her in a year," Papa stated, just now remembering he had one.

"Papa, she's been dead for some time now, her body was scattered and dismembered all over Mexico." Mark's voice saddened because it was something he hated to speak about.

"Sorry to hear that."

"It's life, but I'm glad you're here, because I need to tell you something." Mark's facial expression got serious.

"Bad news, I see."

"I found out who killed Mojoa. That's the good news."

"Who?" Papa didn't give a fuck, he planned to kill their whole family.

"El Bien," Mark said, seeing Papa's shocked look.

"Fuck, but why? He was good to us." Papa knew killing a man like El Bien came with a price tag.

"I don't know, but I need you to find a hitman, someone good so we can take him out." Mark saw Papa nod his head and he smiled, knowing his plan would work.

Romell Tukes

Chapter 40

183rd, The Bronx

Staring at the flat screen TV on his bedroom wall, Body couldn't believe what he just saw. A man was found dead with a gunshot wound to his face in a parking garage located in Manhattan yesterday.

Body smiled when he saw his uncle Ice's face pop up on the screen as the victim, he climbed out his king size bed to tell Top the news, plus he needed to holla at his boy anyway.

Cyn surprised him by how fast she got the job done, but if she was so good, why did she need me? They to start to teach through his head.

"Yurroo…." Body said, walking into the living room to see Top and Mickey in a serious battle on the new PlayStation game.

"Yourro, what's popping?" Top replied, focusing on the game he was losing.

"Brother, watch how I do Top," Mickey said, playing *Basketball 2K* dunking all over Top's team.

"Shit," Top shouted down by ten points.

"Top, let me holla at you real quick," Body stated.

"Hold on, I can't let this little nigga beat me." Top was getting serious as Mickey laughed at him while scoring point after point.

"You can play that shit all day," Body said as Top paused the game.

"This shit better be good." Top followed Body into the kitchen away from Mickey.

"Ice dead."

"What, already?"

"Yeah, I just saw him on the news. One of my people owed me offer." Body kept it short and simple, but Top caught his drift.

"Oh ok, so we lit now, niggas got move on Steel and Montay."

"Yeah, but I need to go handle something else real quick so I'm be focused on another situation."

"I'm almost outta work, bro. niggas got like twenty-four birds left Gage been going crazy, bro. Facts."

"What's up with King H?" Body asked, happening he wasn't fucking up the money.

"His young boys on it. They getting to a bag still, but he went MIA, son," Top said, hoping his boy was ok.

"I'm pull some strings, bro. Facts," Body said, thinking if should go in the stash or hit a lick.

"What y'all talking about?" Mickey asked, entering the kitchen the kitchen to grab a snack and juice.

"None of your business," Top said.

"Come back to the game so I can bust you up," Mickey taunted, asking Top and making a mean face. Top and Body both laughed.

***

Burnside, The Bronx

The summer brought everybody out in the best gear, from the classy chicks to a ratchet chicks. Today there was a big block party for a few fallen soldiers and a hood legend name Dru everybody loved doing a life term sentence in the feds.

"Gage and his crew was out post on the strip getting high, dancing to music, drinking and having a good time. Gage loved hood day because a gang of new Bitches would show up from all over the city.

"Yo son, niggas brought the bikes out," Hekoo said, seeing a gang of bikes do all types of tricks up and down the block showing off. The police didn't even bother to stop them or the RV's.

"That's Lil RN and Kegjay,'' one of Gage's soldiers started, watching one of the chicks walk up the block with her ass hanging out.

"Nigga trying out tonight?" Gage asked his crew who always brought out the bag and made a movie everywhere they went, including city events.

Gage was proud of his team for getting off the scamming shit and chasing a real bag. His whole crew drove in nothing but Benz, BMW, Maserati, and Hellcats. This was the life Gage dreamed of since he was a little nigga on the block selling nicks.

Being a gangsta wasn't Gage's story but he wasn't a punk either, getting money was his thing since he was a youngin. When Top came to him with the offer, Gage thought his boy was Top's cousin, he knew there was no such thing as the word family in the streets.

"Ayo Gage, who that in the black BMW?" E baby said.

Gage looked to his left and that's when shit run haywire.

TAT....

TAT....

TAT....

TAT....

TAT....

TAT....

TAT....

Gage felt a pain hit his shoulder as he went for his gun to shoot back at the BMW. Two of Gage's men hit the ground.

Boc....

Boc....

Boc....

The crowds of people ran all over the place as the BMW raced off, and Gage took a back block with a few of his shooters who were nowhere to be found when the gunfire took place.

"I saw that Montay nigga," Larry T said, outta breath from running. As they all stopped near Harris Street. Gage looked at his shoulder, but it was only a small graze. He was thankful the bullet missed, unlike a few of his people.

Romell Tukes

Chapter 41

Spanish Harlem, NY

The city tried to close down Papa's restaurant since the shooting took place a few weeks back, but he knew some people in higher places that helped him keep the establishment.

Papa sat in the back office, watching the video over and over from beginning to end, trying to figure out who the young man was that robbed him outta twenty bands. Three days before the incident took place, Papa felt as if he needed to switch up all his stash spots, which he did the next morning.

Whoever hit the restaurant had to know something and this worried Papa because someone would know more. The kid found dead in the basement, next to a female employee and his security guard, name as Curt. Asking around, Papa's people found out Curt was a low life thief, in and out of jail always looking for a come up.

The other kid was who Papa wanted the most. He must admit, the young man was smooth. The way he clipped Curt and left no trail let Papa know he wasn't a rookie or a dummy. One big fatal mistake the kid made though, was not wearing a mask.

***

Body laid back in his new car he copped today since Ray got killed in his white Charger, so he bought a Maserati fresh off the lot.

Waiting for Papa to come out felt like forever. He'd been following his victim since he left a condo apartment downtown. Body had to admit Papa was a sick nigga, he busted at least four drug moves on his way to the restaurant.

Jalisa called him early to check up on her boys and to once again suggest to Body to lay low. "Maybe get outta town," she told Body. He had a lot of family on his dad's side in Jamaica, which would be a good place to hide out until the Mojoa shit died down. Body already had his mind made up and with niggas like him, there was no changing his mind, even after death.

Scrolling through Hope's social media, he had to smile because she looked beautiful. even famous rappers were stalking her *IG* page. Hope had one point four million followers. Body wasn't really into the whole social media shit, but he had a page he barely posted on because he was too busy and didn't need the feds on him.

Right on cue, Papa came out the restaurant, walking around before making it to the silver Rolls Royce SUV with custom factory rims. Riding in style was something Papa knew how to do and he always did it big.

Body slid outta his car, staying low like a tiger hunting in the jungle on a hungry night. When Papa closed his car door, Body popped up at his driver side window.

Before Papa locked the car doors and started the SUV with the push of a button, they made eye contact before body kissed the kingpin goodbye, something he learned from a Jadakiss song.

BLOC....

BLOC....

BLOC....

BLOC....

BLOC....

Body was in shock, seeing the bullets from his 9mm handgun only put a small dent on the window each round. Papa smiled at Body before racing off, running over his right foot.

"Ahh, fuck!" Body screamed in pain hopping to his car on one foot. This was the first target Body ever missed.

Driving off on his good foot, Body wanted to call Cyn and curse her out for not warning him about the bulletproof glass Papa had.

Since Papa saw his face Body knew it was do or die with no questions asked. So, Body's main focus was now on the old man before he took Body's life.

***

Pace University, NY

Brooklyn walked through campus on her way to Hope's dorm because she called all day long, telling her to pull up so they could talk. Brooklyn really liked Hope and she thought the young lady was perfect, but maybe too perfect for a nigga like her brother, and she hated seeing a good woman get hurt.

For a while now, Brooklyn knew Body was deep in the streets, but she never told Jalisa or anyone else. Instead, Brooklyn prayed he'd be safe and grow outta it, unlike must nigga who died in the streets or went to prison.

This past Sunday was Brooklyn's first time going to church and she loved it, the feeling felt so free and spiritual. Hope's dorm wasn't too far from here, so it didn't take long fo Brooklyn to arrive.

KNOCK....

KNOCK....

"Brooklyn, come in," Hope yelled in an excited upbeat tone.

"Hey," Brooklyn said, seeing Hope jamming to an old 702 album, dancing with herself.

"Sit down, sis." Hope's mood made Brooklyn get excited for a second.

"You ok, Hope?" Brooklyn started to think her girl was high off pills, like must kids on the school campus.

"I'm pregnant," Hope shouted, happier than ever.

"Huh? What? Hold up... by whom?" Brooklyn looked lost.

"By your brother silly, who else?" Hope said, dancing around Brooklyn in circles. Brooklyn sat there dumbfounded, trying to let it all soak in, wondering if Body knew yet.

Romell Tukes

Chapter 42

Castle Hill PJ's, The Bronx

Montay walked into his stripper bitch Pretty Bandz's kitchen, look-ing for something to eat, but her fridge was empty. The only thing he saw was roaches racing around a pan of leftovers.

"Broke bitch." Montay walked back to her room to get dressed, there was no way he could go through the night starving.

Pretty Bandz was up texting but when she saw him appear back inside the room, she swiftly slid her phone and her body under the covers. Montay had been fucking her for a few weeks now and her shit was on fire. He'd been trying for years to fuck, but she used to always tell him to get his money up.

When he pulled up on her in a new drop-top coupe with big chains on, she quickly changed her energy. Every nigga in Castle Hill wanted the thick Spanish, tatted up bitch who had niggas going crazy over her pussy.

"I thought you was sleep," he said, walking into a room grab-bing his denim Armani jeans

"I heard you in the kitchen, so I got up. Plus, I'm hungry." she gave him a look to see if he was going to pay for Door Dash or get some food and go home. "I want some Caribbean food, daddy."

"That sounds good to me." He faked a smile.

"You got some weed on you?"

"You got some money?"

"Damn, it's like that? You know I took off work tonight at Star-lets so we can chill babe." She gave him the sad eyes.

"I'ma bring some back."

"Ok, don't forget and when you came back, I'm signing my name." She laughed, licking her fat lips she was a pro at using.

"Say that." Montay had mixed feelings about coming back now or not.

Leaving the apartment, he pressed the elevator button, forget-ting the shit was broke just like every other building in his projects.

Montay loved his hood, but it was just too nasty, crazy and dangerous.

The horrible news about Ice's death shocked him and Steel. They would have never imagined Ice would be the first to go, and they'd have to penny pitch the little product he had left to the niggas. Montay agreed, but then thought of a get-rich plan himself to find a good lick somewhere, downtown or in the Heights.

One of his boys told him about a Spanish nigga named Papa and Montay planned on doing his research. Checking the time on the bust down AP watch, it read 1:45 am.

Walking downstairs in the stairwell, Montay thought he heard a weird roar from the staircase above. Montay stopped and looked back to see nobody coming down the sixth-floor flight.

The noise grew louder, causing Montay to look around this time, but he still saw nothing. "I'm buggin," said Montay, turning around, walking down the next flight of stairs.

Outta nowhere, King H flew through the fifth-floor doorway, stabbing Monat viciously with a knife the size of a grown man's leg.

Montay tried to push King H off him, but the way his body was pinned to the wall, he couldn't move.

King H stabbed him over hundred times, before he shoved the knife in Montay's forehead with all his force, leaving it there. King H clothes and hands had blood dripping as he smiled, looking at Montay's lifeless body slumped on the staircase, exposing the most gruesome scene he had ever seen.

***

Brooklyn, NY

Body didn't have time for himself, but then Hope asked him to meet her in Brooklyn at the Barclay Center. He was about to say no until she told him it really was urgent.

This was Body's first time here and he liked the place, it was just a lot of people so looking for Hope became a mission itself.

Earlier, Body had awakened to hear about the news of what happened to Montay, and he couldn't believe how dirty someone did him in his own hood. *That was brave*, he thought. Top suggested it was the Cartel who did that to Montay, but Body didn't think Montay was plugged in like that. Whoever took him out, it meant one less person he had to worry about.

Hope was sitting down near the lobby of a restaurant in a nice dress, with her hair all done up, looking cute.

"Hey handsome," she said, giving him a hug.

"Hi babe, what's goin on?" Body could tell Hope just wanted some company.

"Let's sit down and eat first, I'm hungry." She grabbed his hand, leading him to a table.

"This is a nice place." Body looked around.

"Yeah, I saw it online," she admitted.

They talked for a few minutes, then he saw her eating everything from breadsticks to salad, while awaiting their orders. He could tell there was something wrong with her, because she acted strange.

"You good, ma?"

"Huh?"

"What's going on, Hope? You moving funny."

"I'm pregnant," she shouted.

"Really…Oh shit, ma." Body was happy, he reached over to give her a kiss. They talked all night about the baby growing in her. Body was full of smiles and Hope was too.

Romell Tukes

Chapter 43

MDC, Brooklyn

Months Later

Coming back from court was a dreadful feeling for anybody in prison, especially coming from trial. Jalisa sat in the bullpen with her head in her lap, waiting to be led upstairs by the correctional officer.

Today was Jalisa's fourth and last day at trial, but shit didn't go in her favor at all. The twelve-person jury, six males and six females, a mixture of all races came up with a guilty verdict. When the jury came out with the news, she wanted to cry, but could not shed a tear.

When she turned around to look at Body, who was in the second row of the courtroom, he had tears welled up in his eyes. She told him she loved him and wished him a Happy Birthday, because today was his birthday. Jalisa tried not to think about it, but today was also the date her late husband passed.

Jalisa mind was all over the place, but she had to put her game face on before going back upstairs. The next court date was for sentencing. The judge had already told Jalisa she would receive a harsh punishment and seeing daylight was out of the question.

She saw a C.O. open up the bullpen door, a fat dark-skinned woman who had been working there for two decades. Jalisa heard through the grapevine the lady would bring in drugs, phones or liquor, whatever you wanted as long as the money was right.

"Come on, young lady, your ride is here." The C.O. smiled, seeing Jalisa wasn't in a smiling mood.

"Thank you," Jalisa said, entering the elevator with the C.O.

"You're the queen pin chick who just blew a trial, right?"

"It's written on my forehead or something?" Jalisa couldn't believe how fast word spread, but nothing surprised her these days.

"Nah, it's all over the news honey, you're a star in here."

"Sometimes being a star ain't worth the fame," Jalisa stated as the elevator stepped.

"Tell me about it. But I been watching you on camera inside the unit and I like your style. When you go back to your unit, the C.O. going have a bed roll for you, and I'm pretty sure you're a smart young lady," the guard said before letting Jalisa off on her floor.

"Good night," Jalisa told her before walking off to the unit door.

Inside the noisy unit, Jalisa handed the C.O. a tall, skinny, pretty brown woman her ID.

"How was court?" her regular unit C.O. asked

"I'm still trying to figure that out," Jalisa shot back sucking her teeth.

"You will be ok, keep faith, every dog has their day. Here is your bedroom. It's getting a little cold in here... but have a good night." The C.O. was always respectful and humble when dealing with the prisoners, unlike most guards who would talk down to them.

Jalisa walked to her cell, seeing women staring at her, wondering where she had been, because a lot of women go to court to snitch. Only a few saw the news covering her trial today and for the past four days. Most prisoners had been on the same unit for five to ten years, waiting for the people they snitched on to go to trial, so they could take the stand for a lesser charge or freedom. Some women were really fighting serious cases and standing tall, not going out like suckers.

Once in the cell, she covered the window. She figured Marylean was upstairs in the chapel, at church tonight as always on Thursdays. Jalisa undid the bed roll and two brand-new iPhones with SIM cards and chargers laid there, next to a Ziploc bag full of weed, pills, coke, K-2 and bundles of heroin. The jail price of everything in front of her had to be worth eighty to a hundred thousand.

There was a note that said, "Send five thousand cash to this *PayPal* Tiff Bandz, and be safe." Jalisa planned to have Body send the money tomorrow. She knew he was depressed due to her losing at trial, but she needed him to be strong because he is all she got.

Her mom's trial starts next week, and the lawyer said it wasn't looking good on her behalf.

***

South Bronx

This day was the worst day of the year for Body, unlike most people who celebrate their birthday, but he hated it because today was the day he lost Moss. Body remembered it like yesterday, the day Moss got gunned down in broad daylight.

Body waited for his father all day it seemed like at his birthday party, but when Moss never showed up, things got awkward. Even Jalisa couldn't figure it out as she called her lover back-to-back.

The moment the news hit, Jalisa broke down in tears right in front of the whole party. That's when young Body knew something was wrong.

Climbing out the car, it was a little cold, and cold chills ran through his body before he grabbed his coat out the back. Body came to visit his dad's graveside, something he did every birthday.

Walking to his father's tombstone, carrying fresh flowers, Body thought he was bugging when he saw a female with long silky hair, wearing a peacoat and heels, standing there. with long silky hair.

Before Body went within ten feet of the lady, she put her left hand up. She felt his presence a mile away and today she knew he would come here as he did every year on this day.

"There is a lot to me you don't know, Nick." The female voice sounded too familiar, but when she turned around Body was left speechless.

"Cyn, what's going on?"

"Happy Birthday and it's a long story, a story you may not ever understand." Cyn looked back to her first lover's grave, the man she would always worship and love.

Body tried to take it all in, but he gained a headache trying to make sense of this, because why would Cyn have any ties to his dad?

"You need to start talking. I don't know what type of weird games you're playing, but you got five minutes." Body pulled out a pistol and pointed it at her face, but she didn't seem bothered by it at all.

"Me and Moss used to be an item. I was the side bitch and Jalisa was his everything, but I understood that, so I played my role. Your father saved my life more times than I can imagine but when it was time for me to save his, I couldn't." Her eyes got glossy.

"What you mean?"

"Moss and me were partners. I was a hit woman in Puerto Rico. Your father found me and put me to the test. The biggest one was Papa, the man who Mark sent to murder your father. Me and your dad were supposed to kill both of them, but we both got comfortable with time. I've been plotting all these years how to get them back and we will. I have to go, be in touch soon." Cyn just walked off. Body couldn't believe what he just heard. For years he was wondering who killed his dad, now he could breathe and kill them all.

Chapter 44

New York City, NY

Papa smoked on the expensive cigar, in deep thought as two big guards stood outside the smoke room for his own protections inside the smoke lounge. Since being in the game, Papa had never had to have twenty-four-seven security with him.

Since the shootout in front of his restaurant, Papa hadn't been able to sleep, knowing someone almost completed an attempt on his life. Luckily the Rolls Royce SUV was the only automobile that was custom-made bulletproof.

That day he was going to take his Lambo, but it was supposed to rain. Papa couldn't get the kid's eyes outta his head, they looked familiar as if he had seen them before.

He needed to find out who would want him dead, all types of thoughts ran through his brain, but Papa did so much dirt it was hard to pick. Right now, he had to focus on protecting his and Cyn's lives. Papa was ready to ask the beautiful woman to marry him, but he wanted the drama to die down.

A cell phone tone took him outta his zone, seeing it was his, Papa picked up the call from Mark, his boss. "Yes, boss?"

"Where are you at?" Mark asked with a light, panicked tone.

"The smoke lounge next to 39th Street."

"We have a problem, Papa."

"What happened?" Papa put his burning cigar out hoping to save it for later.

"El Bien is on a private jet here, right with his men."

"No, can't be." Papa couldn't believe it.

"Yes…Who did you tell our plan to, Papa? Something isn't right." The real white boy started to come outta Mark because he was scared to death.

The only time El Bien came to the states was to personally kill someone or kill groups of people in his way of getting product in the states.

Mark and Papa watched El Bien wipe out a whole Cuban Cartel and many Mexican Cartel families, trying to move into Texas, Miami, and of course the East Coast.

"Mark, I swear, I haven't told a soul. You know me better than that." Papa tried to cover his own ass, but he knew better than to tell anybody about the suicide mission he agreed to.

"Did you find anybody for this job yet?"

"I'm still looking," Papa lied. he went to three well known assassins from Mexico, trying to get them to take the offer to kill EL Bien, but once they found out how the target was all three quickly declined.

"You moving slow but he wants just one there when he lands in an hour." Mark heard the other end get quiet.

"Us as in me too?" Papa asked a dumb question.

"Yes… and be normal because if he smell some fishy shit, we both dead."

"Ok."

"Meet me at JFK in thirty minutes," Mark said before hanging up.

Papa saw his hands shaking outta fear and anger. He was about to be face-to-face with a longtime friend, and the man he believed killed his brother.

***

JFK Airport, Queens

El Bien's door opened to his private jet and eight goons stepped off first, checking the surroundings, a limousine waited for their boss and two SUVs for them.

On the far left stood Mark and Papa, awaiting the big boss to get off the jet

Stepping off the jet, El Bien wore a heavy white suit on this chilly day, taking a deep breath of fresh air then looking to Mark and Papa, whom he hadn't seen in years.

"My friends, join me," El Bien said, walking towards the Bentley limousine awaiting him.

Mark and Papa both followed his lead inside the large limo, with TVs and a bar inside.

"That's a nice suit, El Bien, it's been a while," Papa said, putting on a fake smile. The three sat in the back as the limo pulled off, with two of El Bien's goons in the front.

"Yes, it has, my friend, and you look the same." El Bien laughed.

"Years of good sex and food." Papa made everybody laugh.

"Yes, I see. And I'm sorry to hear 'bout Mojoa, he was a good kid," El Bien said, seeing Papa's face tighten. Mark looked at Papa, hoping El Bien didn't catch on to Papa's expression.

"I'ma find his killer," Papa said through his teeth.

"You have my help if needed," El Bien said, pouring three glasses of champagne.

"What brings you to New York? I can't remember the last time you were out here," Mark spoke for the first time seeing El Bien smirk.

"Wouldn't you like to know?" Bien looked at Mark, then out the limo's tints, loving the beautiful but dangerous city.

"Of course," Mark added, accepting the drink El Bien handed to him, thinking whether his boss poisoned the drinks already for a quick kill. He knew El Bien loved to watch a slow death.

"I came to see a friend and also take care of some unfinished business. May we toast to that?" El Bien lifted his glass and they followed, praying neither one of them was his unfinished business. But they had a feeling something big was about to go down real soon.

Romell Tukes

Chapter 45

Soundview, The Bronx

Top had been calling Gage's phone since he woke up, because last night Top gave him twenty-five keys to sell, and shit had been a drought for two days. Yesterday, Gage called him crying, talking about how he needed product, now he was nowhere to be found.

Luckily, Top had to go towards Burnside anyway, then pick up an outfit from Fordham, to go out this weekend with a bad little bitch he met in Harlem the other day. Body told him about the Cyn chick and that whole story sounded crazy.

Since they were youngins, he knew about Body's second life as a contract killer. He found it cool but crazy at the same time, especially for his best friend to be on that type of time.

Nobody would ever expect a person like Body, who was humble, quiet, and kindhearted to be a hitman. Top always thought hit men were strictly for the mobsters not blacks, especially in The Bronx, but he was wrong.

While driving he called Gage's phone one more time before he popped up on his block unannounced. Top hung up after hearing the voicemail again. He hoped Gage wasn't locked up. Gage also owed him a lot of money. He prayed his cousin didn't play him outta all that money, because half of it was Body's paper.

All of a sudden, his mind shifted to King H. He hadn't seen him in months, every day he worried more and more about him, hoping at least God was protecting King H. Top knew how close King H and his mom was, so he knew her death took a toll outta his boy.

King H's soldiers had been running Highbridge since their boss' disappearance, and they were raking in big bucks still, as if King H was present. Top planned to drop of twelve kilos to Gage and the rest to King H was present Top planned to drop off twelve kilos to Gage and the rest to King H people in Highbridge.

Cruising down Burnside, he peeped two of Gage's young boys in front of the corner store, chilling on milk carts.

"Ayo, where Gage at, son?" Top rolled down the window to his Audi coupe.

"Oh shit, what up Top?" DB acted as if he really knew Gage's cousin but only saw him twice.

"Ain't shit, trying to find my cousin."

"He was at his baby crib in the building next door to that nursing home, it's 3F. We all went out to New Jersey last night and got crazy in the strip club. I'm broke as hell right now," Big Choppy said, tapping his pockets.

"Not for long, you'll be straight in a few hours," Top told them both.

"Aight say that, big homie." DB nodded his head knowing Top was about to flood the hood.

"Go figure," Top said to himself now knowing why Gage's phone was off, he was still asleep from partying. Top needed to speak with his cousin about partying so much right now in the time of war. Everybody knew he was a show-off and loved being in the spotlight because he never was, but Top planned to tell him to turn it down a little.

Trying to be that nigga in a city like New York would only get you two things. One would be a fresh lick for a jack boy to rob and kill. The second would be having the feds round up your whole crew, raid crack houses and end niggas' careers. Top didn't like either option, so he needed to have a sit-down today.

Top's baby mother Donada was a hood thot. He disliked her because she only fucked with niggas for their money. Gage was the lucky dumb nigga to get caught slipping now he had to deal with her for eighteen years. Word in The Bronx was, Donada had that snap back that made her ex kill himself over her, when he found out she as creeping with his father.

Top found the building and went upstairs, surprised at how new and clean the complex was. Gage's old apartment building was nasty, full of mice, and right in the hood, this building seemed more low-key.

He knocked a few times to get no answer.

"This goofy nigga" Top mumbled, turning around to leave, but something in his mind said use the doorknob and he did just that. The door slowly opened as he stepped in.

"Gage… Donada…Yo Gage, where you at?" he yelled, only to hear a TV playing, coming for the back room.

Top saw kid's toys all over, diapers, a box of pizza, two empty bottles of Henny and Gage's black Timbs. Top made it to the back room to see the door was cracked open.

"Gage?" Top whispered, sticking his head inside the room but the scene he saw almost made him vomit.

Gage and Donada's naked bodies laid on top of her bed, covered in blood, both with bullet holes in their upper torsos.

Top saw a baby's leg sticking out from under the bed, he knew it had to be his baby cousin. When Top grabbed the baby's leg, that was all he held in his hand, a part of the small baby. Top saw another leg and arm belonging to the baby on the other side of the bedroom.

Top couldn't stand to see anymore, he rushed out, he'd never seen such crazy shit like that. Top was against killing kids because they were innocent to life, but whoever did this seem to think different.

***

183rd, The Bronx

Since Mickey went to the movies with his friend, Body wanted to catch up on some sleep, because shit's been draining him mentally and physically overall. Body started to wonder what it would be like to have a normal lifestyle.

The more he thought about it, the more Body knew the circumstance he was faced with in life was already prepared. Plus, his grandma Ms. Dee was a gangsta, Jalisa and Moss were gangstas, so the thought of being a gangsta was already awaiting its moment since he was a kid.

Body remembered his first kill. He felt nothing, pulling the trigger felt normal, that's when the murder high kicked in.

Laying down about to doze off, it didn't last long as Body jumped up out his sleep like a commando gripping his FN handgun after hearing a loud slam. He heard Top's voice as he exited his room, so he calmed down, seeing Top walking circles in their living room.

"You good, bro?" Body asked.

Niggas kill Gage and his BM."

"What? When?"

"I don't know. I just left there, and they were all dead, including the newborn. Son, this shit is fucked up." Top punched the wall out of anger, feeling as if it was his fault his cousin was dead.

"Relax, bro. Let's go to Miami for a few days and get our minds right, bro." Body suggested, thinking about leaving Mickey in Brooklyn with their cousins.

"We out." Top went to pack a bag, still pissed off.

Chapter 46

Miami, FL

The next evening, Body and Top got off their first-class flight, feeling like they were in a different world because New York was experiencing a snowstorm today, while Miami was in the high seventies.

"I'm glad we came out here, bro," Top said, as he walked outta the airport, trying to wave down a cab as if he was still in New York City.

"Shit, we both needed this time, bro. I was starting to speculate I might have been on my way to losing my mind." Body laughed, but he had a lot on his plate.

"Facts, son. Quality time is unheard of nowadays."

"That's the ultimate sacrifice to the game I've realized."

"Ironically, my nigga, I wouldn't give this life up for nothing."

"Top, you're a no-good ass nigga, of course this life is perfect for you," Body joked as they got in the cab, telling the Cuban driver to take them to the best hotel in Miami.

After twenty minutes of driving around, Body felt something was odd because the last time he came it only took ten or less minutes to get to the hotel.

"Where are we going, to Disneyland?" Top joked, wondering why the drive was going all through different areas of Miami.

Top had never been out to the 305, but he saw it on the *First 48* crime show, and the area he saw looked familiar from TV.

"Papi, it's no hotel over here, take us to South Beach," Body shouted as the cab driver looked over his shoulder, smiled and nodded his head.

"Yo, bro. I don't think he speaks English," Top said as the cab made a right down a street connected to West Miami.

Body saw a suspicious glance from the cab driver in the rearview mirror. It didn't take a rocket scientist to peep the man had something up his sleeve.

Body then remembered killing Mojoa and all types of thoughts raced through his head, upset with himself for not having a weapon.

"When the car stops, get out and run," Body whispered in Top's ear.

"Huh?" Top looked confused, not catching on.

"Nigga, at the next stop sign... run," Body scolded. Then the cab driver hit the child locks and turned into a parking lot. Finally, they came to a halt and the Cuban man spun around with a gun.

"Don't yell, run, or try anything. I will kill you." The cab driver spoke perfect English, getting out to open their door, lowering his weapon as they climbed out looking up at the tall complex.

"You finna kill us do you," said Body, showin no signs of fear as Cuba smiled.

"If she wanted you dead, you would have been dead." Cuba lost him by his statement, leading them into the back way.

"This some bullshit," Top fumed.

"Just play it cool, son." Body acted brave but in reality, he felt more scared than Top.

On the top floors of Miami University, there were signs everywhere.

"Sit in the living room and don't touch nothing." The Cuban man give Top a watchful look.

"This place is nice." Top slipped his hand on expensive vases and class in paintings.

"A female lives here." Body looked around, admiring the place because whoever lived there had class and a lot of money.

"Yes, I live here." A pretty Spanish woman with long hair in a ponytail, rocking a college sweatsuit approached them both.

"Damn she fire." Top whispered.

"Excuse me?" she said, looking at Top, rolling her soft hazel eyes that caught every man's attention.

"Nothing," Top said, seeing the Cuban man come back out from the hallway.

"Should I stay?" the Cuban man asked the young woman.

"No, everything is fine, thank you so much," she replied with no worries. The big Cuban man gave both men a mean look before leaving out to handle his business.

"Who are you?" Body never saw her a day in his life, but he could tell she was his age or younger.

"That's a good question, but I'll save that for last. How about we start off with why you're here, Body?" she said.

"She knows your name, bro," Top told him, trying to be discreet.

"I know your name is Top, but this isn't really about you. Sorry, you're just the tagalong here." She laughed at her own joke neither one of them found funny. "Take a load off, sit down, your life is safe for now." She took a seat on the white leather couch.

"You still ain't answer the question," Body stated, still standing.

"Ok sure, you are not the best contract killer in New York. At first, I thought it was a joke. I mean, look at you. You're handsome, but I don't see a killer bone in your body." She made Top giggle.

"It's good to know," Body shot back, not taking offense to her rudeness."

"But when I saw you kill Mojoa, I had a newfound respect for you, especially since he was Jalisa's plug." Her words made Body uncomfortable.

"Look ma, I'm not for the games, so tell me what you want or I'm out." Body started to get pissed hearing his mom's name.

"Calm down there, I mean no type of disrespect. Me and you got a lot in common, trust me. But I just wanted to meet you face-to-face, that's all," she said.

"Most people call, text, or *FaceTime* when they wanna meet someone. You went above and beyond to bring us here. How the fuck did you een know we was coming?" Top cut in.

"I'm different and I know a lot." She looked at Body and smiled.

"You're a fucking kid, how do you know all this?" Body had to question her.

"I'm nineteen and I go to college out here."

"It's clear you have the wrong person," Body said.

"You can play that game but soon, you'll need me like I need you," she said.

"I never needed nobody."

"You'll be surprised at how fast life changes for good and worse." She stood up.

"What's your name?" Top asked.

"Everybody calls me Heaven."

"Cute name for a nice college girl," Body said, ready to leave.

"There's a reason why they call you Body, right?" she gave him a wink before walking them to the door.

"You got a man?" Top tried to shoot his shot.

"You're not my type at all, stink breath."

"I'll see you around, Heaven," Body told her while walking out the apartment.

"Sooner than you think."

Chapter 47

Westchester County, NY

Being back in New York sucked, but Body couldn't stay on vacation as much as he wanted to, things needed to be taken care of back home. The whole trip, Body could not stop thinking about Heaven because she'd said a lot of things, but so many people knew about it and he needed to get to the bottom of it fast.

Driving down State Street in Ossining, a small town, he drove past a prison called Sing Sing, which faced the Hudson River. Seeing the prison made him think about his mom and grandma doing prison time.

The moment he heard the judge say Jalisa would most likely be spending the rest of her life behind bars, Body's eyes got watery. He'd never been to jail but could only imagine how it could break a person, mentally and emotionally, if people let it.

Parking in front of the yellow brick house that belonged to Hope's family, he saw her coming out in a North Face coat looking very cute. Hope took a break from school so she could focus on a healthy pregnancy. Staying at her family's house was perfect, it's better than being in The Bronx where she grew up and Brooklyn. As a kid, Hope and her family moved around a lot because her mom and dad were both in the Army so whenever they were deployed somewhere, Hope would stay with other family members.

"Hey, Mr. Miami," Hope stated with a slight attitude, climbing into the car.

At first, Body didn't tell Hope he went out to Miami, he assumed she would be a little jealous or try to stop him. Top posted a picture of him and Body at Club Liv, and she called Body seconds later spazzing, calling him cheaters, a liar, and a bunch of weirdos.

"Where is the doctor's office at?" Body asked, ignoring her slick comment. Today was Hope's first doctor appointment, so he wanted to be there for her.

"White Plains." Her whole vibe screamed attitude. Body pulled off, paying it no mind.

"You hungry?" Body broke the awkwardness in the car.

"I ate this morning, but I want to apologize for the way I acted the other day. That was very immature of me." Hope looked in his eyes.

"I understand but it's my fault too for not telling you. I just got a lot on my plate."

"Yeah, I already know, that's why I felt bad. But this pregnant shit be having me super emotional," she admitted.

"It's regular."

"Yep, so tonight you gonna let me suck that dick?"

"Shit, we can do that now" Body was already horny, looking at her thighs and sexy lips.

Hope wasted no time in sucking her man off the whole ride to the doctor's appointment in White Plains, she was just glad he didn't crash.

***

MDC, Brooklyn

Ms. Dee sat quietly in the rec room upstairs alone, threading a bunch of yarn together, making long jump ropes for the inmates who used them to work out with daily.

Yesterday, Ms. Dee lost her trial on three murders she was silent the whole time at trial trying to understand her own fate. But when the lawyer informed her about Jalisa blowing her trial, Ms. Dee already had her mind on losing.

Even though Jalisa wasn't her co-defendant, her cases were much worse than Jalisa's drug offenses. Since leaving court, Ms. Dee hadn't said a word to anybody because she had nothing to say.

Back in the day, Ms. Dee was a known killer and drug dealer, running with all the big dawgs of New York from Brooklyn A-Team to the Harlem Rick Porter days. She was a legend only few know about. Deep down, Ms. Dee loved the life she used to live, but looking at it now, it wasn't worth it one bit.

Checking the time, it was 3:00 pm, thirty minutes left until count time, so she went back to her cell to use the restroom. After she took a piss, Ms. Dee wrapped a thick, homemade rope she'd made inside the vent air hole six times, before tying a large-sized loop at the bottom.

"May the Lord protect my loved ones," were her last words, before she placed her neck in the rope's loop, climbing on the chair then jumping off.

The guards walked around to do count and saw Ms. Dee lifeless body hanging from a rope she sewed together days ago already plotting her own death.

***

Jalisa laid on her bunk listening to old Mary J. Blige, one of her favorite R&B artists, on the MP3 player prisoners had to buy for eight dollars plus buy songs for. Marylean was on visit, so this was Jalisa's quiet time. The unit was all locked in for count, so the place was silent.

Since blowing trial, Jalisa came up with the logic that this would be her new home, until a blessing came when she would be let free. But, counting on that was less likely.

The bang on her room door caught Jalisa's attention, making her snatch the headphones out.

"Yeah?" She saw the officers and the prison chaplain at her door.

"You're Jalisa?" the old white chaplain asked.

"Yes, but I don't want to attend service this week," she told the creepy looking man, before turning around.

"It's not that," one of the correctional guards said from behind.

"What is it?" Jalisa saw sad faces.

"Your mom has committed suicide and we need to speak with you" the priest said in slow motion, rubbing his cross and thinking about the two photos of her young boys, she had on the table. The priest couldn't help but stare at the handsome young men he wished he could have to do nasty things with.

"Say that again." Jalisa hoped her ears hadn't heard right.

"Your mother just took her own life, and we need…" The priest stopped explaining when Jalisa walked over to her bed to sit down.

Something about the way her mom had been acting lately had made Jalisa uncomfortable. But never did she imagine the strong independent woman who raised her would take her own life away with no remorse.

Chapter 48

Jackson PJ's, The Bronx

Blick and Green Eyes kept a good enough distance on their target, who pulled the Audi coupe into Jackson Projects, a known dangerous area to most.

"Can we just get this shit over with?" Green Eyes said in the passenger seat clutching a .45 handgun, with thirty-two shots in the long clip.

"Nah son, we gonna do what the boss said. Have patience, let's not fuck this bag up." Blick gave his partner in crime an odd look, but Green Eyes already know what it was for.

Blick and Green Eyes were contract killers from Harlem who would kill for a few bands if offered. They been working together for five years, so slip ups were meant to come along. The last mistake was the biggest slip yet. Green Eyes mistakenly chose the wrong target and killed him across the street from Yankee Stadium. That wasn't the worst part, come to find out the victim Green Eyes killed was an off-duty cop, so he went to hide out in Boston for two months.

Freshly back two weeks, his boy Blick had a new project lined up for them from an old head named Papa. He put down forty grand a piece on Top's head and the nigga who tried to kill him at his restaurant. Papa had cameras outside of his food spot, so he was able to get a good look at Body's face. Papa gave Blick two photos of the men, and he found Top with ease, but Body was still in the works.

"Shit happened, but whoever put that money up must really want his nigga." Green Eyes watched Top step out the Audi to embrace some tall nigga with dreads.

"Facts, but I can care less. For forty K, I'll kill my mama," Blick said, staring at Top.

"Damn, you cold. I need at least a hundred K to kill mama luv."

"Head tap and all that?" asked Blick.

"No doubt." Green Eyes laughed but was serious while watching Top's every move.

***

Top came to speak with a nigga named Grip who just came home from do a seven-year bid update for armed robbery. Top and Body knew Grip from Soundview where he was raised but when he started moving around the BX, making a big name for himself.

"Welcome home, my G," Top said.

"You know that strap, but I been hearing a lot about you out here in dees streetz."

"Regular shit, I'm out here trying to win."

"Facts, but what's up with King H? I ain't seen the bro since I been out," asked Grip because he and King H went way back since Rikers Island days, going to war with the Brooklyn niggas over chairs in the dayroom, on the minor block.

"I haven't seen him in a few months to be real, you know son lost his mom and bro ain't been right since."

"Damn the homie's moms was good people. She used to send me thirty-five-pound food packages up north daily. Son." Grip sounded sad because King H's family were good to him off the strength of King H, they treated Grip like they own.

"What's your plan now you out?" Top asked slowly, getting to his reason of coming to this side of town.

"I'm tryna get like you."

"Robbery?"

"By any means, bro. You know how I give it up, my nigga." Grip smiled.

"The whole Bronx do, but seven years is a long time and shit different out here now, bro."

"So, I see." Grip looked at the Audi coupe.

"I want you to get money with me and my crew, while most of the team died or disappeared," Top corrected himself.

"Selling what?"

"Keys."

"Damn, you stepped your shit up, what the nigga Body doing?"

"The same thing as me, we are a team, bro," Top stated, not trying to take all the shine.

"Aight, let me build a team in Jackson, Michell, Cortlandt, Millbrook, and Castle Hill. Since Montay gone, I'm just muscle my way in plus I got people all over."

"Bet, let's get this money, I'm waiting for your call."

"Say that, give me three days." Grip pulled out his phone walking off, making calls to take over the city.

Driving back home, Top hoped putting Grip down with his crew was a good idea and he would be loyal to the squad, because Top knew firsthand turning a jack boy into a dope boy wasn't an easy task.

Pulling up to the spot, Top saw a truck pass him that's been on his ass since getting off the exit, but now it passed he relaxed. Top just want to make something to eat, shower, and take a nap. Top wanted to start going to the gym but he's too busy plus tired.

Rushing to the kitchen, he only saw deli meat, bread, chips, soda and frozen chicken.

"Damn, nigga's gotta go shopping," Top said, pulling out apples from the bottom drawer, hearing a door crack but the paid it no mind as he was just focused on grubbing.

"Make one fucking move, son. I'll knock that weak ass hairline back, bitch," a man with green eyes said.

"I know you gotta gun on you," Blick said, patting Top down, finding two twin Desert Eagles on him.

"Nice pair," Green Eyes said.

"I don't even know y'all niggas," Top said, knowing he got caught lacking in his own crib. Body was with his sister, breaking the bad news to her about their grandma's death.

"Does it matter who the fuck we are, nigga? We here to kill, dummy." Green Eyes laughed hard.

"Whoever sent you two must know what I am," Top said, seeing both gunmen's faces frown.

"You must not know who we are, little nigga. Harlem World finest," Green Eyes got hyped as he always did before pulling the trigger.

"Why Papa put forty K on your head, so you must be some-body," Blick said about pulling the trigger.

"Papa?" Top asked himself, trying to think where he had the name from. Then it clicked, the robbery with Curt in Spanish Harlem.

BLOC....

BLOC....

BLOC....

BLOC....

Top waited for his body to drop from the gunshots, but nothing happened. Green Eyes' body hit the floor first, then Blick fell right after in slow motion. Both men suffered head shots. Top couldn't believe this shit... Mickey held the smoking gun, looking at the two men.

"What the fuck? Give me that." Top snatched his gun he kept in the living room from Mickey, in complete shock. he just saved his life and killed two niggas with clean head shots.

"Just like *Call of Duty*," Mickey said smiling.

"Go pack your shit and come on," Top yelled, knowing they had to leave before more gunmen came. Top called Body so he could explain what happened.

Chapter 49

MDC, Brooklyn

Jalisa had been spending most of her time in the cell, trying to sleep the days away until sentencing, then being transferred to her prison somewhere in the mountains.

Marylean sat at the desk drawing a picture, something she did to burn time and was really nice at.

"What's that?" Jalisa asked, seeing Marylean draw a big house with perfect detail.

"My home."

"You lived there?" Jalisa was shocked because Marylean didn't seem to have a lot of money.

"Don't look so surprised, there is a lot you don't know about me, Jalisa. I am telling you a quick story of why I'm here, just because I genuinely like you and I know you're not a rat like these stank bitches in here. I left Colombia and moved to New York to pen a bigger empire for me and my brother, because I think big. I went to war with all types of cartel families for turf like Texas, Miami and New York. My brother used to come out here to watch me kill other cartel families to steal the glory. I ended up meeting a man and marrying him. I swear, Jalisa, the man didn't have a penny. I made him rich, him and his brother Mojoa."

"Mojoa?" Jalisa sat up.

"Let me finish, my love. So, I married Papa and introduced him to my brother, and they formed a cool bond, until a man name Mark came in the picture. Mark's a Spanish Puerto Rican guy who looks white. My brother used Mark as his face so he could play the backhand, trying to snake me out of my shit due to his greed. Ten years passed and my husband, Mark and my brother all set me up, snitching on me to the FBI about murders, drug trafficking, and extortion. Before my arrest, I met a man in New York who I heard was the best killer the city had to offer." She paused, taking a deep breath reflecting on her story.

"The man's name was Moss, but when I got arrested some years later, Papa killed him. Mark and my brother must have got wind of who killed Moss." Marylean saw Jalisa with tears brimming in her eyes as her hands shook uncontrollably.

"Moss was my husband."

"I know, my love, and you will forever be rewarded on my behalf." Marylean held Jalisa's hand.

"You knew this whole time?"

"Yes, for years I've known who you are. My reach is still long, but now I'm hoping to give my time back because they fucked up on my case."

"Does Mark own banks?"

"Yes, the ones you worked for," Marylean said, seeing the dumbfounded look on Jalisa's face.

"I shoulda known."

"Mark received a special gift from me before I came to jail because I saw this coming. So, I killed Mark's beautiful wife and dismembered her body. That was my little going away gift," Marylean said smiling.

"Wow, this is crazy."

"Food for thought, my love." Marylean walked out the room to send an email, even though Jalisa got her a phone.

Jalisa sat on her bunk in deep thought, trying to piece everything together. The whole time Mark, and Mojoa's brother Papa, had been the missing pieces to the puzzle. She knew Mark had to be on her line since having Moss killed, that's why he came to the funeral and gave her a job promotion. Now Jalisa had to put a plan of revenge together, with Body's help, who was coming tomorrow anyway to visit her.

Body showed up on time as usual, waiting for Jalisa to come out to inform her of the good news about Hope being pregnant. He waited until this day to inform her because Body wanted to tell her in person. This would be the first visit since his grandma died so he wanted shit to go right.

In a matter of seconds, Jalisa came out and walked right up to her son, gave him a big hug and whispered something his ear. "Kill them all, everyone, I mean today." She then sat down.

"I'm having a child."

"Who? Oh my God, baby, I'm so happy for you."

The news shocked Jalisa, but Ms. Dee used to always tell her, "When one go, another one comes into this world."

"Yeah, you're about to be a granny"

"A young granny, get it right."

"My bad." Body loved seeing his mom smile.

"How's Mickey? I spoke to Brooklyn this morning."

"He's good," Body lied, not wanting to stress her more by telling him he killed two people.

"Take care of them, please."

"I will."

"Listen, the man who killed your father, his name is Papa. A man named Mark sent him, but they both work for a man named El Bien, he's from Colombia. Find these people before they find you, son. Mark owns banks all over the city, the one I used to work at also. I know what you do, so I'm trying to point you in the right direction," she spoke in a low-pitched voice.

"Two steps ahead of you."

"I don't understand." She looked confused.

"I'm handling it." Body didn't want to tell her he knew most of the shit she told him, but he wanted to ask how she found out all that shit.

"Call me tonight," she said, seeing a C.O. getting ready to end the short visit.

"Do you know a young lady named Heaven from Miami?"

"No, I don't believe so, why?"

"Oh, nothing, just asking."

"You sure?" Jalisa questioned.

"Yes. I love you, be safe."

"Love you too, but being safe is in good hands, staying dangerous in your control, son." Jalisa hugged Body and left him sitting there putting his own game plan together with the names and info he just gathered.

Chapter 50

Cortlandt, The Bronx

Months Later

Steel had just gotten picked up for a murder charge from nine years ago, and a fresh gun charge to add with it because when they pulled him over claiming it was a traffic violation the pistol was on his passenger seat.

On the ride to the police station next to Cortlandt Projects, they informed him about a murder. Steel had been sweating bullets as they threw him into an interrogation room in cuffs.

Two black detectives walked in. "If it isn't the big bad Steel, how you been nowadays?" Detective Mason asked, pulling up a chair.

"Who did that to your big homie Ice," Detective Lance said, trying to pick Steel's brain, but he played it cool, trying to conceal his fear.

"Man, I don't know who or what y'all talking 'bout, fam," Steel shot back.

"Your uncle, the top shotta whose head was found blown off and from the looks of it, he fucked with the wrong person, playa." Detective Mason looked at Steel, handing him a photo of Ice's crime scene.

When Ice saw the gruesome head photos, he wanted to throw up, but he took a deep breath and looked forward.

"Never saw him."

"Ok fair, but I bet you saw this person, because you're the one who killed Shaw G'z from Mott Haven Projects. New evidence links your DNA to the crime scene, buddy." Detective Lance handed him a picture of Shaw G'z and Steel's face said it all.

Steel remembered Shaw G'z clearly. Ice wanted the young man dead because he stole twenty thousand dollars of Ice's money. Instead of getting his hands dirty, Ice sent his nephew who was new to street view at the time. Eager to earn his storms in the street, Steel killed Shaw G'z in his own building, where no cameras were.

"You got the wrong person."

"Steel, we can *First 48* you, break you down until you start to sing like R. Kelly in this bitch," Detective Lance said.

"Or we can listen to your side of the story. Lower the charge to an assault, get you a two-to-four bid in exchange for the people who you've been beefing with that have been leaving a trail of bodies all over the city," Detective Mason finished his partner and undercover lover's sentence.

"If I give you the person who is responsible for all this shit, I get cut," Steel asked.

"We ain't say all that, brother man. But we will work something out to get you a lesser charge." Detective Mason saw his words were getting to him.

"This shit can't get back to the streets with my name on it or I'ma be another Apollo in the hood." Steel knew too many official niggas who ratted and fucked up their legacy.

"Your secret is as good with us," Detective Lance looked at Mason.

"Ok, the nigga is from Highbridge, his name is King H." Steel saw the two D's look at each other.

"I knew it," Detective Mason shot because in two of his information meetings, his name came up a few times.

"Let's find this cocksucker," Detective Lance shouted.

***

Pace University, NY

Three Months Later

Brooklyn walked outta her last class for the day exhausted, thinking about laying in her bed. Dealing with the death of her grandma and Jalisa blowing trial, the stress started to overcome her mentally.

With Hope being pregnant, due any day and outta school, she had no friends to bother or vent to, so Brooklyn was holding shit inside.

People flooded the campus, a lot of new faces and old people she spoke to, here and there. Back at the dorm she saw an older Spanish man lurking, watching her every move, giving Brooklyn the creeps.

"Weirdo," Brooklyn stated to herself, pulling out her keys to the apartment, knowing her roommate always locked the door before going to work.

Looking at the door latch, she saw it was cracked open, with the doorknob loose. She slowly opened the door and saw two shadows with guns appear.

"Oh, hell no," Brooklyn shouted, taking off running as two Spanish men with guns busted out of the apartment, yelling in Spanish as they chased Brooklyn.

The man that was watching her jumped out, firing at her.

BOC....

BOC....

BOC....

BOC....

BOC....

BOC....

Brooklyn ducked, but felt a sharp pain enter her left leg, slowing her down as students started screaming and yelling at another school shooting. Brooklyn hit the floor and two gunmen quickly ran down on her.

"Little bitch," one of them said before aiming his pistol.

BOOM....

BOOM....

BOOM....

BOOM....

Brooklyn's eyes were shut tight. She slowly opened them to see King H standing over her after he killed both men, but he saw more coming his way.

"Come on, we gotta ago," King H said, helping her up. Making their way to the parking lot, they forced their way through the chaos.

"What the fuck is going on?" she yelled, leaping to her car.

BOC....

BOC....

BOC....

BOC....

"People trying to kill you!" King H snapped, dodging the shots

BOOM....

BOOM....

BOOM....

BOOM....

King H hit one of the shooters in the parking lot.

"That's my car." Brooklyn pointed ten feet away in front of them, but bullets were coming from everywhere.

"Get in your car and drive off," he told Brooklyn, firing back at more shooters as two detectives' cars arrived but they looked like they were coming for him.

***

"There he go right there, can you believe this shit?" Detective Mason said in his walkie talkie, to chance flying into the parking lot where the shooting was taking place with their target.

The detectives had been watching King H's moves for a few days now, waiting on the perfect time to take him down. When they arrived at the college, they were confused as to what he had up his sleeve, until they saw two vans of Spanish gunmen jump out, concealing the weapons patrolling the campus.

"We got his ass now," Detective Lance said, almost hitting King H with his car, but instead left two skinny white college kids fearing for their lives.

***

King H saw Brooklyn drive off and jumped in his new Hellcat Red Eye he got for events like this. The detectives were only a few feet away when he cranked the gas pedal. Bullets hit the car from every angle but King H laughed, driving on the campus grass, avoiding the traffic jam of student trying to escape the madness taking place.

The cops were still in his rearview when he flew over speed bumps, on his way to the back entrance close to a highway. The Hellcat took off, slamming into two police cars trying to block its path.

King H was loving the show as he bust a right, flying down a main street, dipping in and outta lanes to avoid car accidents.

A line of cop cars was in the rearview mirror but the Hellcat had a big lead on them. King H called Body, keeping one hand on the steering wheel.

"Yo, who that?" Body answered, not knowing the new phone number.

"It's King H, bro."

"Oh shit, yo! What the fuck, bro? You good, my guy?" Body was shocked to hear from him.

"Yeah, I saved her. I've been watching, a nigga named Papa is out for you." King H saw the police were getting close to him so he busted a U-turn, going back the other way, fucking up the police's train of thought and making the cop car crash.

"What's all that noise?"

"It's a long story, bro, but make sure my name lives on, homie. Tell Top I love him, this is it for me," King H said, seeing a roadblock with spikes on the floor.

Before Body could reply, the cell phone hung up. King H hit his brakes, picking up the new, fully loaded AR-15 assault rifle on the floor.

"Fuck it. I'm the last of a dying breed," King H said hopping out with the weapon, opening fire at his enemy, the law.

TAT....

TAT....

TAT....

TAT....

TAT....

TAT....

King H hit one officer in the face before a line of cops riddled King H's body with bullets, making his body do a dance, before spinning and dropping. Detective Mason was the first one to cheer as he took the kill shot.

"Get this piece of shit outta here," Detective Lance yelled, standing over King H's dead body in the middle of the street his co-workers had closed off.

"Fake ass Blood," Detective Mason said, before spitting on King H's lifeless body.

"This nigga musta been into it with some powerful people," Detective Lance said, walking to his car.

"Let's go check the scene out at the college. I got a feeling shit is a little deeper than we seeing."

"Me too, them Mexican cats looked like cartel members or some shit," Detective Lance said.

"I got a feeling it's about to get ugly... and who was that chick King H was trying to protect?" asked Mason.

"We about find out."

"After all this hard work, I'ma need a treat." Detective Mason gave his partner a look they both knew too well.

"I got you tonight, daddy gonna stretch you out." Detective Lance whipped past other cops.

"I'ma call my wife and tell her I'll be home late."

"Yes, you will." Detective Lance smirked and climbed back in his car, heading back to the college to gather up evidence.

Chapter 51

Mount Vernon, NY

Body met up with Brooklyn at a car wash in Mount Vernon to make sure she was ok. He parked right next to his sister's Lexus and saw how hard she was crying.

"You straight?" Body snatched her driver's door open, seeing how shaken up she was and scared.

"Some Mexicans or Spanish people came to my school with guns, trying to kill me, and some dude I saw with Top before saved my life," she managed to say through deep breaths.

"You're safe now. Take these keys and go to my crib in Yonkers by the waterfront, 5G. Hope should be there." Body handed her the keys so he could go link up with Top because he knew Cyn would bring him to his enemy. Body remembered Hope should be dropping their baby boy any day now, so he had to take care of Papa and make his way back home.

"Where are you going?" she asked.

"Nowhere. I'ma be back in a little bit, you'll be safe there."

"Ok, love you," she said, wiping her tears.

"Love you too." Body pulled out his phone rushing to his car about to call Cyn, but a call from Hope came in first.

"Hello, babe. I'm on my—"

"My water broke. I'm on the way to the hospital now," Hope yelled in pain.

"I'm on my way, where are you?"

"Babe, meet me at White Plains Hospital, hurry."

"Where are you now? I'm coming for you," Body said, driving back to Yonkers running stop signs.

"I'm in an Uber."

"Ok, I'll meet you there, love you." Body was more than excited.

"Love you more." She hung up.

***

Yonkers, NY

Hope had called for an Uber the second her water broke, knowing Body was attending to Brooklyn, who was caught in the school shooting. Before her water broke, Hope was home watching the breaking news about the school shooting and a man who shot it out with police, not too far from the college campus.

She couldn't believe all the mayhem that was going on. She was glad she wasn't at the college because four students were pronounced dead and Hope knew one of them.

"Having a boy or girl?" the Uber driver asked.

"A boy." Hope held her stomach in pain, praying the hospital was closed because she wasn't familiar with the Yonkers or White Plains area.

"That's a blessing, huh?" The old man smiled.

"Yes, how far are we?"

"Not too far, a few minutes. Just sit tight, little lady," the driver said.

"Oh my God!" she screamed in pain as the car pulled into a park. "You making fucking pit stops, man? I'm in labor, you asshole," Hope shouted.

"That's no way to talk to the man who's gonna choose your fate." The driver hit the brakes and jumped out the car, opening Hope's door, dragging her out by her long hair to the ground.

"Help!" she screamed.

"Body isn't here to save you now." Papa put his gun to her head.

BOC....

BOC....

BOC....

BOC....

BOC....

BOC....

Papa emptied his clip into Hope's upper body, then said a short prayer. Hearing her phone ringing inside the car took him away from his focus. Papa saw the name "My Babe," pop across the caller ID and picked up the phone.

"Babe, where are you at, the hospital?" Body yelled though the speaker.

"My friend, she is no longer her with us, but for all its worth someone send you, was it El Bien?" Papa asked, climbing back in his car, leaving the park nobody ever came to.

"If you touched her, I'm killing everything you love," Body's voice sounded crushed.

"I don't doubt you will kill everything I love but there is a secret. I don't love a soul because I don't have one, and first you gotta find me." Papa tossed the phone out the window before getting on the nearest exit, leaving the state.

***

Manhattan, NY

Six Months Later

Mark had to do some paperwork at one of his banks before going to New Jersey so he could speak with a woman who birthed his son over twenty years ago, but he'd kept it hidden from the world.

Today he was gonna drop her off some money. He'd made a trip overseas because he felt like the past year had been hacked and stressful.

"Boss, I'm going home, do you want me to lock up?" a young white woman approached his office door.

"Yes, please."

"Have a good night." She walked off as Mark continued his paperwork, ready to leave himself. It. was 8:20 pm.

Ten minutes later, Mark started to pack up his things until he heard a footstep, causing him to look up.

"Don't move a muscle," Body said, holding one of his employees in a chokehold, aiming his gun at Mark.

"Just chill, the money is in the safe upstairs." Mark thought it was a robbery until the young man laughed and shot the employee in her head, tossing her frail body to the wall. Mark knew whoever the man was, he wasn't to be played with.

"Why you got my father killed?" Body asked.

"You must be Moss' son."

"Live and present."

"Moss was sent to kill me, so I did what I knew best." Mark's words were truthful.

"Respect but you killed the wrong nigga, Mark, because my father started to like you. So, he paid Cyn to kill you." Body saw the look on Mark's face.

"Well, that's new kid, but look, we can't go back in time. So how about we take a moment and think about business. I'll pay you four million in cash, if you let me walk out of here alive."

"Mark, you're good, but not that good," Body said, pulling the trigger.

BLOC....

BLOC....

BLOC....

BLOC....

BLOC....

Mark's body flew into the chair, dying with his eyes wide open as if he saw it coming. Body felt a little weight lifted off his shoulder, but he still had a hit list to complete.

Leaving the bank, he put his hoodie over his head then outta nowhere, a metal object came cracking down on the back of his head, knocking Body unconscious before he was dragged inside a van.

***

Fishkill, NY

Body opened his eyes, trying to get his thoughts back together of what happened and why he felt a head rush. Looking around, Body saw a lot of tools as if he was in someone's shed.

"Sorry you had to experience that blow but I had to be discreet somewhat," a female voice said, walking into the shed with a plate of cooked food.

"Where am I?"

"At my mansion in the guest house shed," the lady stated.

"Who are you?" Body saw how beautiful and curvy the woman was and couldn't help but stare.

"Body, I'ma good friend of your mother, and you're in danger, some pretty bad men are out for you."

"How do you know and what makes you think I would trust you?" Body asked, seeing her smile.

"These people used to be close to me, and I'm all you got," the stranger said before a breeze touched the back of her neck, making her turn around.

BLOC....

"Wrong, he got me," Heaven said, dressed in all-black seeing Body's puzzled face. "We have to go... her goons are everywhere."

"Wait, who sent you and what is going on?" Body looked at the woman then back to Heaven.

"I'm Cyn's sister, but I'll explain everything to you, son. Let's go now." Heaven saw goons approach the shed from the window.

Heaven fired her way outta there, killing six trained shooters, taking Body to a safe location to explain to him what was going on.

To Be Continued...
Bronx Savages 2
Coming Soon

Lock Down Publications and Ca$h Presents assisted publishing packages.

BASIC PACKAGE $499
Editing
Cover Design
Formatting

UPGRADED PACKAGE $800
Typing
Editing
Cover Design
Formatting

ADVANCE PACKAGE $1,200
Typing
Editing
Cover Design
Formatting
Copyright registration
Proofreading
Upload book to Amazon

LDP SUPREME PACKAGE $1,500
Typing
Editing
Cover Design
Formatting
Copyright registration
Proofreading
Set up Amazon account
Upload book to Amazon
Advertise on LDP Amazon and Facebook page

***Other services available upon request. Additional charges may apply

Lock Down Publications
P.O. Box 944
Stockbridge, GA 30281-9998
Phone # 470 303-9761

Submission Guideline

Submit the first three chapters of your completed manuscript to ldpsubmissions@gmail.com, subject line: Your book's title. The manuscript must be in a .doc file and sent as an attachment. Document should be in Times New Roman, double spaced and in size 12 font. Also, provide your synopsis and full contact information. If sending multiple submissions, they must each be in a separate email.

Have a story but no way to send it electronically? You can still submit to LDP/Ca$h Presents. Send in the first three chapters, written or typed, of your completed manuscript to:

LDP: Submissions Dept
Po Box 944
Stockbridge, Ga 30281

DO NOT send original manuscript. Must be a duplicate.

Provide your synopsis and a cover letter containing your full contact information.

Thanks for considering LDP and Ca$h Presents.

NEW RELEASES

OUL OF A HUSTLER, HEART OF A KILLER 2 by SAYNOMORE

SOSA GANG by ROMELL TUKES

PROTÉGÉ OF A LEGEND 2 by COREY ROBINSON

BRONX SAVAGES by ROMELL TUKES

Bronx Savages

STRAIGHT BEAST MODE III

De'Kari

KINGPIN KILLAZ IV

STREET KINGS III

PAID IN BLOOD III

CARTEL KILLAZ IV

DOPE GODS III

Hood Rich

SINS OF A HUSTLA II

ASAD

YAYO V

Bred In The Game 2

S. Allen

THE STREETS WILL TALK II

By Yolanda Moore

SON OF A DOPE FIEND III

HEAVEN GOT A GHETTO II

SKI MASK MONEY II

By Renta

LOYALTY AIN'T PROMISED III

By Keith Williams

I'M NOTHING WITHOUT HIS LOVE II

SINS OF A THUG II

TO THE THUG I LOVED BEFORE II

IN A HUSTLER I TRUST II

By Monet Dragun

QUIET MONEY IV

EXTENDED CLIP III

THUG LIFE IV

By **Trai'Quan**

THE STREETS MADE ME IV

By **Larry D. Wright**

IF YOU CROSS ME ONCE III

ANGEL V

By **Anthony Fields**

THE STREETS WILL NEVER CLOSE IV

By **K'ajji**

HARD AND RUTHLESS III

KILLA KOUNTY IV

By **Khufu**

MONEY GAME III

By **Smoove Dolla**

JACK BOYS VS DOPE BOYS IV

A GANGSTA'S QUR'AN V

COKE GIRLZ II

COKE BOYS II

LIFE OF A SAVAGE V

CHI'RAQ GANGSTAS V

SOSA GANG II

BRONX SAVAGES II

By **Romell Tukes**

MURDA WAS THE CASE III

Elijah R. Freeman

THE STREETS NEVER LET GO III

By **Robert Baptiste**

AN UNFORESEEN LOVE IV

BABY, I'M WINTERTIME COLD III

By **Meesha**

QUEEN OF THE ZOO III

Bronx Savages

By **Black Migo**
A GANGSTA'S PAIN III
By **J-Blunt**
CONFESSIONS OF A JACKBOY III
By **Nicholas Lock**
GRIMEY WAYS III
By **Ray Vinci**
KING KILLA II
By **Vincent "Vitto" Holloway**
BETRAYAL OF A THUG III
By **Fre$h**
THE MURDER QUEENS III
By **Michael Gallon**
THE BIRTH OF A GANGSTER III
By **Delmont Player**
TREAL LOVE II
By **Le'Monica Jackson**
FOR THE LOVE OF BLOOD III
By **Jamel Mitchell**
RAN OFF ON DA PLUG II
By **Paper Boi Rari**
HOOD CONSIGLIERE III
By **Keese**
PRETTY GIRLS DO NASTY THINGS II
By **Nicole Goosby**
PROTÉGÉ OF A LEGEND III
By **Corey Robinson**
IT'S JUST ME AND YOU II
By **Ah'Million**
BORN IN THE GRAVE III

By Self Made Tay

FOREVER GANGSTA III

By Adrian Dulan

GORILLAZ IN THE TRENCHES II

By SayNoMore

THE COCAINE PRINCESS VII

By King Rio

CRIME BOSS II

Playa Ray

LOYALTY IS EVERYTHING III

Molotti

HERE TODAY GONE TOMORROW II

By Fly Rock

REAL G'S MOVE IN SILENCE II

By Von Diesel

Available Now

RESTRAINING ORDER **I & II**

By **CA$H & Coffee**

LOVE KNOWS NO BOUNDARIES **I II & III**

By **Coffee**

RAISED AS A GOON I, II, III & IV

BRED BY THE SLUMS I, II, III

BLAST FOR ME I & II

ROTTEN TO THE CORE I II III

A BRONX TALE I, II, III

Bronx Savages

DUFFLE BAG CARTEL I II III IV V VI

HEARTLESS GOON I II III IV V

A SAVAGE DOPEBOY I II

DRUG LORDS I II III

CUTTHROAT MAFIA I II

KING OF THE TRENCHES

By **Ghost**

LAY IT DOWN **I & II**

LAST OF A DYING BREED I II

BLOOD STAINS OF A SHOTTA I & II III

By **Jamaica**

LOYAL TO THE GAME I II III

LIFE OF SIN I, II III

By **TJ & Jelissa**

BLOODY COMMAS I & II

SKI MASK CARTEL I II & III

KING OF NEW YORK I II,III IV V

RISE TO POWER I II III

COKE KINGS I II III IV V

BORN HEARTLESS I II III IV

KING OF THE TRAP I II

By **T.J. Edwards**

IF LOVING HIM IS WRONG…I & II

LOVE ME EVEN WHEN IT HURTS I II III

By **Jelissa**

WHEN THE STREETS CLAP BACK I & II III

THE HEART OF A SAVAGE I II III IV

MONEY MAFIA I II

LOYAL TO THE SOIL I II III

By **Jibril Williams**

Romell Tukes

A DISTINGUISHED THUG STOLE MY HEART I II & III

LOVE SHOULDN'T HURT I II III IV

RENEGADE BOYS I II III IV

PAID IN KARMA I II III

SAVAGE STORMS I II III

AN UNFORESEEN LOVE I II III

BABY, I'M WINTERTIME COLD I II

By **Meesha**

A GANGSTER'S CODE I &, II III

A GANGSTER'S SYN I II III

THE SAVAGE LIFE I II III

CHAINED TO THE STREETS I II III

BLOOD ON THE MONEY I II III

A GANGSTA'S PAIN I II

By J-Blunt

PUSH IT TO THE LIMIT

By **Bre' Hayes**

BLOOD OF A BOSS **I, II, III, IV, V**

SHADOWS OF THE GAME

TRAP BASTARD

By **Askari**

THE STREETS BLEED MURDER **I, II & III**

THE HEART OF A GANGSTA I II& III

By **Jerry Jackson**

CUM FOR ME I II III IV V VI VII VIII

An **LDP Erotica Collaboration**

BRIDE OF A HUSTLA **I II & II**

THE FETTI GIRLS **I, II& III**

CORRUPTED BY A GANGSTA I, II III, IV

BLINDED BY HIS LOVE

Bronx Savages

THE PRICE YOU PAY FOR LOVE I, II ,III

DOPE GIRL MAGIC I II III

By **Destiny Skai**

WHEN A GOOD GIRL GOES BAD

By **Adrienne**

THE COST OF LOYALTY I II III

By Kweli

A GANGSTER'S REVENGE **I II III & IV**

THE BOSS MAN'S DAUGHTERS I II III IV V

A SAVAGE LOVE **I & II**

BAE BELONGS TO ME I II

A HUSTLER'S DECEIT I, II, III

WHAT BAD BITCHES DO I, II, III

SOUL OF A MONSTER I II III

KILL ZONE

A DOPE BOY'S QUEEN I II III

TIL DEATH

By **Aryanna**

A KINGPIN'S AMBITON

A KINGPIN'S AMBITION **II**

I MURDER FOR THE DOUGH

By **Ambitious**

TRUE SAVAGE I II III IV V VI VII

DOPE BOY MAGIC I, II, III

MIDNIGHT CARTEL I II III

CITY OF KINGZ I II

NIGHTMARE ON SILENT AVE

THE PLUG OF LIL MEXICO II

CLASSIC CITY

By **Chris Green**

Romell Tukes

A DOPEBOY'S PRAYER

By **Eddie "Wolf" Lee**

THE KING CARTEL **I, II & III**

By **Frank Gresham**

THESE NIGGAS AIN'T LOYAL **I, II & III**

By **Nikki Tee**

GANGSTA SHYT **I II &III**

By **CATO**

THE ULTIMATE BETRAYAL

By **Phoenix**

BOSS'N UP **I , II & III**

By **Royal Nicole**

I LOVE YOU TO DEATH

By **Destiny J**

I RIDE FOR MY HITTA

I STILL RIDE FOR MY HITTA

By **Misty Holt**

LOVE & CHASIN' PAPER

By **Qay Crockett**

TO DIE IN VAIN

SINS OF A HUSTLA

By **ASAD**

BROOKLYN HUSTLAZ

By **Boogsy Morina**

BROOKLYN ON LOCK I & II

By **Sonovia**

GANGSTA CITY

By **Teddy Duke**

A DRUG KING AND HIS DIAMOND I & II III

A DOPEMAN'S RICHES

Bronx Savages

HER MAN, MINE'S TOO I, II

CASH MONEY HO'S

THE WIFEY I USED TO BE I II

PRETTY GIRLS DO NASTY THINGS

By Nicole Goosby

TRAPHOUSE KING **I II & III**

KINGPIN KILLAZ I II III

STREET KINGS I II

PAID IN BLOOD **I II**

CARTEL KILLAZ I II III

DOPE GODS I II

By **Hood Rich**

LIPSTICK KILLAH **I, II, III**

CRIME OF PASSION I II & III

FRIEND OR FOE I II III

By **Mimi**

STEADY MOBBN' **I, II, III**

THE STREETS STAINED MY SOUL I II III

By **Marcellus Allen**

WHO SHOT YA **I, II, III**

SON OF A DOPE FIEND I II

HEAVEN GOT A GHETTO

SKI MASK MONEY

Renta

GORILLAZ IN THE BAY **I II III IV**

TEARS OF A GANGSTA I II

3X KRAZY I II

STRAIGHT BEAST MODE I II

DE'KARI

TRIGGADALE I II III

Romell Tukes

MURDAROBER WAS THE CASE I II

Elijah R. Freeman

GOD BLESS THE TRAPPERS I, II, III

THESE SCANDALOUS STREETS I, II, III

FEAR MY GANGSTA I, II, III IV, V

THESE STREETS DON'T LOVE NOBODY I, II

BURY ME A G I, II, III, IV, V

A GANGSTA'S EMPIRE I, II, III, IV

THE DOPEMAN'S BODYGAURD I II

THE REALEST KILLAZ I II III

THE LAST OF THE OGS I II III

Tranay Adams

THE STREETS ARE CALLING

Duquie Wilson

MARRIED TO A BOSS I II III

By Destiny Skai & Chris Green

KINGZ OF THE GAME I II III IV V VI

CRIME BOSS

Playa Ray

SLAUGHTER GANG I II III

RUTHLESS HEART I II III

By Willie Slaughter

FUK SHYT

By Blakk Diamond

DON'T F#CK WITH MY HEART I II

By Linnea

ADDICTED TO THE DRAMA I II III

IN THE ARM OF HIS BOSS II

By Jamila

YAYO I II III IV

Bronx Savages

A SHOOTER'S AMBITION I II

BRED IN THE GAME

By S. Allen

TRAP GOD I II III

RICH $AVAGE I II III

MONEY IN THE GRAVE I II III

By Martell Troublesome Bolden

FOREVER GANGSTA I II

GLOCKS ON SATIN SHEETS I II

By Adrian Dulan

TOE TAGZ I II III IV

LEVELS TO THIS SHYT I II

IT'S JUST ME AND YOU

By Ah'Million

KINGPIN DREAMS I II III

RAN OFF ON DA PLUG

By Paper Boi Rari

CONFESSIONS OF A GANGSTA I II III IV

CONFESSIONS OF A JACKBOY I II

By Nicholas Lock

I'M NOTHING WITHOUT HIS LOVE

SINS OF A THUG

TO THE THUG I LOVED BEFORE

A GANGSTA SAVED XMAS

IN A HUSTLER I TRUST

By Monet Dragun

CAUGHT UP IN THE LIFE I II III

THE STREETS NEVER LET GO I II

By Robert Baptiste

NEW TO THE GAME I II III

Romell Tukes

MONEY, MURDER & MEMORIES I II III

By **Malik D. Rice**

LIFE OF A SAVAGE I II III IV

A GANGSTA'S QUR'AN I II III IV

MURDA SEASON I II III

GANGLAND CARTEL I II III

CHI'RAQ GANGSTAS I II III IV

KILLERS ON ELM STREET I II III

JACK BOYZ N DA BRONX I II III

A DOPEBOY'S DREAM I II III

JACK BOYS VS DOPE BOYS I II III

COKE GIRLZ

COKE BOYS

SOSA GANG

BRONX SAVAGES

By Romell Tukes

LOYALTY AIN'T PROMISED I II

By Keith Williams

QUIET MONEY I II III

THUG LIFE I II III

EXTENDED CLIP I II

A GANGSTA'S PARADISE

By **Trai'Quan**

THE STREETS MADE ME I II III

By **Larry D. Wright**

THE ULTIMATE SACRIFICE I, II, III, IV, V, VI

KHADIFI

IF YOU CROSS ME ONCE I II

ANGEL I II III IV

IN THE BLINK OF AN EYE

Bronx Savages

By **Anthony Fields**
THE LIFE OF A HOOD STAR
By **Ca$h & Rashia Wilson**
THE STREETS WILL NEVER CLOSE I II III
By **K'ajji**
CREAM I II III
THE STREETS WILL TALK
By **Yolanda Moore**
NIGHTMARES OF A HUSTLA I II III
By **King Dream**
CONCRETE KILLA I II III
VICIOUS LOYALTY I II III
By **Kingpen**
HARD AND RUTHLESS I II
MOB TOWN 251
THE BILLIONAIRE BENTLEYS I II III
REAL G'S MOVE IN SILENCE
By **Von Diesel**
GHOST MOB
Stilloan Robinson
MOB TIES I II III IV V VI
SOUL OF A HUSTLER, HEART OF A KILLER I II
GORILLAZ IN THE TRENCHES
By **SayNoMore**
BODYMORE MURDERLAND I II III
THE BIRTH OF A GANGSTER I II
By **Delmont Player**
FOR THE LOVE OF A BOSS
By **C. D. Blue**
MOBBED UP I II III IV

Romell Tukes

THE BRICK MAN I II III IV V
THE COCAINE PRINCESS I II III IV V VI
By King Rio
KILLA KOUNTY I II III IV
By Khufu
MONEY GAME I II
By Smoove Dolla
A GANGSTA'S KARMA I II III
By FLAME
KING OF THE TRENCHES I II III
by **GHOST & TRANAY ADAMS**
QUEEN OF THE ZOO I II
By **Black Migo**
GRIMEY WAYS I II
By Ray Vinci
XMAS WITH AN ATL SHOOTER
By Ca$h & Destiny Skai
KING KILLA
By Vincent "Vitto" Holloway
BETRAYAL OF A THUG I II
By Fre$h
THE MURDER QUEENS I II
By Michael Gallon
TREAL LOVE
By Le'Monica Jackson
FOR THE LOVE OF BLOOD I II
By Jamel Mitchell
HOOD CONSIGLIERE I II
By Keese
PROTÉGÉ OF A LEGEND I II

By Corey Robinson
BORN IN THE GRAVE I II
By Self Made Tay
MOAN IN MY MOUTH
By XTASY
TORN BETWEEN A GANGSTER AND A GENTLEMAN
By J-BLUNT & Miss Kim
LOYALTY IS EVERYTHING I II
Molotti
HERE TODAY GONE TOMORROW
By Fly Rock
PILLOW PRINCESS
By S. Hawkins

BOOKS BY LDP'S CEO, CA$H

TRUST IN NO MAN

TRUST IN NO MAN 2

TRUST IN NO MAN 3

BONDED BY BLOOD

SHORTY GOT A THUG

THUGS CRY

THUGS CRY 2

THUGS CRY 3

TRUST NO BITCH

TRUST NO BITCH 2

TRUST NO BITCH 3

TIL MY CASKET DROPS

RESTRAINING ORDER

RESTRAINING ORDER 2

IN LOVE WITH A CONVICT

LIFE OF A HOOD STAR

XMAS WITH AN ATL SHOOTER

Bronx Savages

CPSIA information can be obtained
at www.ICGtesting.com
Printed in the USA
LVHW041833240223
740361LV00001B/77